SEVERAL
DEATHS
LATER

Also by Ed Gorman

ROUGH CUT
NEW, IMPROVED MURDER
MURDER STRAIGHT UP
MURDER IN THE WINGS
THE AUTUMN DEAD

Tobin Mysteries

MURDER ON THE AISLE

SEVERAL

DEATHS

LATER

≈

Ed Gorman

ST. MARTIN'S PRESS ≈ NEW YORK

Design by Judy Stagnitto

Library of Congress Cataloging-in-Publication Data

Gorman, Edward.
    Several deaths later.

    I. Title.
PS3557.0759S4   1988   813'.54   88-15832
ISBN 0-312-02279-4

First Edition

10 9 8 7 6 5 4 3 2 1

For Brian DeFiore
who proves that good editors
can also be good friends

SEVERAL DEATHS LATER

1 Tuesday: 10:43 P.M.

It was while she was slathering her rather nice twenty-eight-year-old body with a bar of moisturizing soap that she got the idea for the letter and she started composing it immediately. Not literally, of course—she was after all taking a shower, and writing underwater was a trick she'd never mastered—but figuratively. Figuratively she started immediately.

She'd use her best stationery—the baby blue with the monogram at the top—and she'd write with the special Cross pen her mother had given her for her last birthday and she'd send the letter to Aberdeen, the plump secretary she worked with at the life insurance company—Aberdeen sort of lived vicariously through her. The letter would read:

> I don't know if you remember the TV show several seasons back called "High Rise" but I just thought I'd let you know that its handsome star (now host of the game show "Celebrity Circle"), Ken Norris, can rise just as high as you might think (if you get my drift).
>
> Aberdeen, it's my first night on the *St. Michael* cruise ship, and I'm already in love with a TV star—and I think he's really interested in me, too! More sordid details later!

Then she'd add, as a tease: "But please don't tell anybody!" knowing that with Aberdeen's tendency to blab, she'd probably do everything but announce it over the PA system so that the entire company would hear about it.

Cindy McBain went back to slathering.

Much as she was excited, she was nervous. Right outside her bathroom door sat TV star Ken Norris himself. Waiting. For her. Cindy was staying in what they called a Mode 4 cabin aboard the gigantic superliner, which meant it had the same sort of severe look the motel rooms of her business college years did, which meant that all Ken Norris had to amuse himself with were those glossy but boring magazines they left in every room. Fortunately, he was pretty drunk—he'd sort of been babbling, matter of fact; and maybe he was taking a short nap.

Cindy had insisted on the shower. She wanted her one and only night with a TV star to be perfect. And that's why she kept slathering, because a TV star like Ken Norris (my God, was he handsome!) would be used to women who served themselves up like pastries. And a lot of work went into pastries. A lot!

As she tilted her head back, letting the water blast at her face, she congratulated herself again for being sensible, for mentioning right in the middle of a kiss what a stickler she was for protection, given all the grave diseases around these days. And promptly he'd waggled a little plastic box at her that listed all the scientific stuff that had been sprayed on to this particular form of latex protection. Why, this stuff would do everything except kill crabgrass!

So, feeling safe now, and feeling clean now, she started to step from the shower, knowing that he was probably tired of waiting for her. The last she'd seen of him, he'd been sitting on the cramped built-in red couch in a black dinner jacket, pouring some more scotch into a drink he said looked "too much like a urine specimen. I like 'em a little darker than this." And looking so dreamy saying it!

She knew that men liked women's hair wet so she didn't do anything more than dry it with a towel and wrap the towel turban-style around her head. Then she stood naked in front of the steamed-over mirror and wiped the critical areas clean so she could get a quick appraisal of herself. For a Kansas City girl who'd never slept with a TV star, she looked—why be unbecomingly modest?—pretty nice. In fact, very nice.

She checked one breast and then the other. They had begun to sag a teensy bit, but sag at least in an interesting way, and then she checked her bottom which had begun, but not so interestingly, to droop, and then she checked her neck, which bore not a trace of impending middle age. She had the neck of a sixteen-year-old.

She was imagining how her second letter to Aberdeen would open when she thought she heard something drop just outside the bathroom door.

Dear Aberdeen,
Don't tell anybody, but he's asked me to come visit him in Hollywood!

He hadn't of course asked her any such thing. But imagine if he did! Imagine if Aberdeen blabbed that throughout the insurance company! Imagine if she got to tell that story at her ten-year high school reunion, which, after all, was coming up in ten months.

Her only concession to modesty was a white terry-cloth robe that smelled cleanly of fabric softener and matched in color and texture the towel on her head. She knew she wouldn't have them on long, anyway.

They'd be heading right for the bed. He'd been ready to go. All ready.

She opened the bathroom door.

The first thing that surprised her was the darkness. He'd apparently turned off the light.

The second thing that surprised her was the quietness—just the soughing and roll of the ocean and the distant sound of a disco band.

The third thing that surprised her was that he said nothing. She shuddered, recalling how, at an insurance convention in Las Vegas she spent the night with this guy who'd taken great delight in jumping out of the shadows and scaring her. Maybe Ken Norris was like that!

The fourth thing that surprised her was when she tripped. It was one of those things you see the Three Stooges do—your arms flailing, your mouth dropping open, your head kicking back—and then you land right on your tush.

Her head landed right next to his head.

She said, "God, you really scared me. You get sleepy or something?"

Nothing.

"I hope you didn't see me trip. I must've really looked stupid."

Nothing.

He just lay there in his dinner jacket, his handsome head turned handsomely toward her.

"Wouldn't you be more comfortable on the bed?" she said.

Then she got this horrible thought.

Maybe he'd been a lot drunker than she'd realized and had simply keeled over. What kind of letter would that inspire to Aberdeen? She'd really have to embroider that one to make it sound like anything at all.

"Why don't you let me undo your tie?" she said. "Maybe that'll make you feel better."

The waves; the roll of the massive ship; the scent of ocean; the cry of birds; her breathing and the wet smell of her hair; and moonlight through the tiny cabin window—she realized then that she was in a place alien to her Kansas ways.

It was because of the moonlight that she finally saw how awkwardly he was positioned on the floor. She just started sobbing softly to herself because it was so ridiculous, just so so ridiculous.

And it ruined utterly—utterly—any sort of decent letter at all to Aberdeen.

Any sort of decent letter at all.

2 11:02 P.M.

Tobin, thanks to the largess of the game show "Celebrity Circle," was spending the cruise in a Mode 5 cabin, which meant he enjoyed the perks of a double bed, a bureau in which to put his underwear with the ragged elastic and the socks that never seemed quite to match, and a somewhat large mirror above the bureau, in which he could assess what forty-two years, red hair, alcohol, any number of fistfights, and the curse of being only five five had done to him.

From the Parade deck he heard the sounds of a band that was made up of lounge lizard rejects from New York—he knew this for sure because they'd bored him in any number of night spots—four guys who all wanted to be Bert Convy when they grew up.

Or was he being unfair, as he was so often unfair?

He decided probably, and he decided to hell with it, and went back to staring at the TV screen.

Thus far he'd not had the idyllic cruise the brochure promised—all that deck tennis, all those voluptuous girls in string bikinis, all those stout chefs pointing to banquet tables filled with colorful decadent food of every kind—no, he'd not had the kind of vacation the brochure wanted you to have, and it was nobody's fault but his own.

The problem was, he was behind in his viewing. Daily, Tobin was bombarded with five to ten VHS videotapes that he'd supposedly view and review for any number of publications. And God, was he behind. Not only had he not seen the new Scorsese; he had yet to see the new Stallone. Not only had Taylor Hackford been overlooked—so had that most celebrated of hacks, Herbert Ross.

Even at this early stage, the voyage had consisted of getting ready to tape segments of "Celebrity Circle" and then immediately dashing back to his cabin for endless goblets of white wine, a cigarillo that he inhaled only occasionally (one couldn't really count this as smoking, could one? Could one?), and grinding through tape after tape on his VCR.

He had learned long ago—and thank the cinema gods for this—to view videos the way New York editors read slush. (Read the first two pages and then start skimming.) All you needed to do was keep your thumb close by the Fast Forward . . .

Amazing how accurate your review could be even though you'd maybe watched—at most—twenty minutes of a ninety-minute film. But then how tough was it to predict the plot of a picture called *Alien Invaders* or *Razor Killer*?

Thundergirls was the name of the video he was watching now.

The biggest problem of the whole process was, of course, staying sober. Easy to keep guzzling and to be drunk before you knew it.

Which is what had happened tonight.

He was potzed enough that even the plot line of *Thundergirls* was difficult to follow.

It seemed to go something like this: there were these three roller-derby girls who were plucked from earth by some strange force and pressed into battle against this creature who lived in a mountain that erupted Vesuvius-like about every five minutes (actually it was the same bad piece of animation played over and over). Or something.

To be perfectly honest, all he cared about was their breasts anyway.

The girls couldn't act (two of them could barely form words), they couldn't move, but by God could they jiggle. They could jiggle wonderfully, marvelously, magnificently, and so what if it was a tatty little picture made by sleazy and cynical morons? By God, it couldn't be all bad, not with breasts like these.

And it was then he realized (a) just how drunk he was and (b) what a great review he could write of this if only his sober courage matched his drunken inspiration.

What if he did a review of *Thundergirls* that said right up front that it was a terrible, incompetent, dull picture but that it was filled with gorgeous breasts? Then he'd proceed to rate the three girls on exactly the basis they should be rated—their looks.

Laughing out loud, already hearing "Sexist!" cried by a chorus of female editors and readers alike, he leaned over, actually sort of collapsed to the right, looking for more wine, and discovered that he had no more wine.

No more wine!

He could no more view videos without wine than he could without a Fast Forward button on his remote control.

He would have to wobble aft and get himself another bottle.

Then he stood up and felt the room spin. Good Lord. He needed air, fresh air, and badly and now.

He left his room immediately.

What he ended up doing, first thing, was strolling about thirty feet down the deck and barfing over the side.

He was careful to lean out as far as he could—there were after all four other decks below him—and in the wind the stuff was rather like orange confetti against the silver moonlight, not unpretty at all.

Then, feeling not only better but infinitely more sober, he began thinking that, after a few blasts of the mouth spray he always carried with him, he might stop in the lounge, have a diet 7-Up, and try his luck. Lay off the wine a bit. And definitely lay off the videos for the night.

A definite spring came into his step; it was, after all, May, wasn't it? And he was aboard a vast and expensive cruise ship in the Pacific, wasn't he? And however much a shit he'd been in the past (whenever he got drunk, he inevitably began thinking of all the ways he'd let down his children, his ex-wife, various girlfriends, his parents, and at least six or seven million other people on the planet)—however much of a shit he'd been in the past, there was no reason to punish himself any more tonight, was there?

No, not any more tonight.

A definite spring came into his step. A definite one.

3 11:06 P.M.

Cindy didn't realize he'd been stabbed until she got him completely rolled over and then got up and turned on the lights and saw the knife sticking out of his chest and the squishy circle of red blood widening with each passing moment.

What struck her first was the ridiculousness of it all. She knew, at least according to all the movies she'd seen, that she was (a) supposed to scream, (b) run terrified from the cabin, or (c) faint.

But actually what she was thinking of was what a wonderful letter this would make to Aberdeen.

Dear Aberdeen,

By now you've probably heard about the murder of that handsome TV star Ken Norris.

Can you keep a secret? He died in my cabin during the cruise. In fact, I was in the shower just before we were supposed to—

Well, I suppose you can fill in that particular blank for yourself, can't you, Aberdeen?

I can't tell you the terrible sadness I feel. Ken and I had become extremely close during the evening we'd spent together. He'd shown me the photos in his wallet (of his 1958 red Thunderbird and his house in Malibu) and I'd told him all about the insurance company and how you and I suspected our supervisor, Mr. Flannagan, of being an embezzler and everything.

But please, Aberdeen, respect my feelings. Please keep this our secret.

Yours sincerely,
Cindy

Aberdeen would be on the company's PA system for sure with this one, and what fame it would be for Cindy. How she'd sparkle among the drab people. A Pacific cruise turning into the murder of a TV star right in her own cabin. It was like Nancy Drew with sex added.

Then she heard the noise behind her, just outside the bathroom, and realized that someone was in the closet next to the bed.

This time she did scream.

This time she did start to feel faint.

She had just reached the cabin door and the corridor when she heard the closet open. Curiosity forced her to turn around for at least a glimpse of the person emerging from behind the racks of Cindy's clothes.

Cindy gasped.

You couldn't tell if it was a man or woman. A black snap-brim fedora and heavy black topcoat with a collar that touched the edge of the hat rushed from the closet into the moonlight and then pushed past Cindy.

"You killed him!" Cindy shrieked. "You killed him!"

But the figure kept moving, not running exactly, just moving steadily away from the closet and out of the cabin.

Cindy knew better than to grab for the person. She did not want to end up the way Ken "High Rise" Norris had. For one thing, she'd be dead. For another, she wouldn't be able to write Aberdeen a letter about any of this.

4 11:16 P.M.

A spring in his step, a tune vaguely inspired by "Rhapsody in Blue" on his lips, Tobin strolled a deserted section of deck thinking of a Dennis O'Keefe movie he'd seen sometime in the early fifties. What made the picture memorable was the starlet in it—so beautiful in memory he dreamed of her still, just as he had when he was seven or eight. She seemed all things impossibly female, and occasionally—as now—he felt real loss thinking of her. What had brought her back was that the picture was set in the South Seas—or at least as much like the South Seas as the Republic Studios back lot could resemble. And being on the cruise (and being potzed) had brought back the O'Keefe picture. Maybe he'd meet somebody like the starlet aboard this ship . . .

The caw of ocean birds; the scent of saltwater; and the wan moon on the wan wash of sea against the rolling boat—how he loved the water and all its myths.

He wanted to call his children and tell them that he was idiotically happy because he was—yes, abruptly and unbelievably, he was indeed happy. The ocean was great therapy for him as it had been for no less than Eugene O'Neill and Stephen Crane and Jack London and Hart Crane—well, check Hart, the man having pitched himself miserably overboard at the end. Wonderful therapy. He wondered how much a ship-toshore call would be, and what time it was in Boston and Los Angeles, respectively.

And it was exactly then that he ran into somebody who was backing out of a cabin.

He assumed she was going for little more than a brief stroll because she wore only a white terry-cloth robe and a towel wrapped around her head.

Beneath the line of her robe he could see that she had sensational legs and as she turned he saw that she had a face to match.

Encouraged by her mere presence—and the elegantly wrought lines of her legs—he started to introduce himself but then he saw that the woman held her hands away from her body, as if they did not belong to her. Or as if she did not want them.

Then he realized that there was a very good reason for this. Her hands and forearms were covered in what appeared to be blood.

"My Lord," he said.

"He's dead. I didn't kill him. Do you think they'll believe me?"

He was so intrigued with her face—very, very nice; an erotic naïveté; or would it be a naïve eroticism—that he said, "Of course they will."

"I don't even own a knife like that."

"Of course you don't."

"And I had no reason in the world to kill him."

"Of course you didn't."

"I just wanted to take a little shower so that our time together would be—well, perfect—and then I came out and found him there. Does that sound believable?"

He was doing his best to peer down the slight opening in her terry-cloth gown, wondrously wound up and ashamed of himself at the same time.

While he was looking at her, she was looking at him and then she said, "You're Tobin, the critic! You're one of them!"

"One of them?"

"One of the panel. 'Celebrity Circle.'"

"Ah. Yes."

"So's he. So was he, I mean."

Then, lust and alcohol receding, Tobin began to have some sense of what was going on here. "In your cabin," he said.

"Yes."

"There's a dead man."

"Yes."

"Stabbed, I believe you said. Or implied."

"Yes."

"And he's—or was, as you said—on the panel."

"Yes."

"My God."

"Exactly," she said, holding her bloody hands out to him as if she wanted him to take them. "And it's not as if he's just another passenger. He's a celebrity. Or was."

The way she said "celebrity"—so dreamily—told him far more than he should have known about her. This glimpse into her both excited and depressed him.

Then, inevitably, he asked, "Who is he?"

"I didn't tell you?"

"No."

"Ken."

"Ken Norris?"

"Yes. 'High Rise.'"

Terrible show, thought Tobin, realizing the curse of being a critic. The poor bastard had just been stabbed and here Tobin was reviewing his show.

"Do you think they'll believe me?" she said again.

"I think so."

"You sounded so much surer before."

"Why don't we go have a look and then I'll call for the captain?"

"God," she said, "Aberdeen will never believe this."

He decided, for the moment, not to ask who Aberdeen might be.

5

11:34 P.M.

Following the murder of his partner, Richard Dunphy—they'd done a TV movie review show together—Tobin had found himself essentially unemployed. The company that owned the show had been sold and the new owner didn't like TV movie review shows at all. "That's sissy stuff," he'd said on the day he'd announced "World Wrestling Wrap-up" as Tobin's replacement—and so Tobin was dispatched to that limbo of late payments, bounced checks, and toadying-to-lessers called "free-lance." There were pieces, and good pieces, if he did say so, for *American Film* and *Cinema* and *Esquire;* there were less good pieces, but far more lucrative, for *Parade* ("Sally Fields' Seven Rules for Being a Good Mother"), and then there was the celebrity circuit.

While Tobin and Dunphy had hardly been famous, at least not exactly, their movie show had played on more than three hundred stations around the country, making it successful, so successful that Tobin's agent was certain that "any day now, babe, we'll be connecting with some moneymen who'll want to not only give you your own show but actually spend some bucks. Truly." Tobin's agent was named Phil Annis, a name that led to all sorts of jokes, in his case deserved. "In the meantime, though," Phil had said, which was how he always preceded news he knew Tobin would hate. "In the meantime, though, I've made a deal with

Cartwright Productions for you to appear on all their basic cable shows. Not much bread, but really good exposure." Cartwright, which Tobin had only dimly heard of, turned out to own five shows: "Celebrity Gardener" (Tobin pretended to be planting roses), "Celebrity Handyman" (Tobin pretended to be building a fancy bookcase, nearly taking off a finger with a SKIL saw), "Celebrity Fitness" (Tobin was seen walking past St. Patrick's Cathedral as the camera grabbed a tight shot of his $250 walking shoes), and "Celebrity Confessions" (a show for which Tobin contrived a tale of being kidnapped at age eight and then left to wander in dark and deep woods for two days before Mommy and Daddy in the family Buick found him alive).

All this nonsense went on for six months before Phil stumbled onto "Celebrity Circle," which was known in some uncharitable quarters as "Celebrity Circle Jerk" and which, if not exactly Hallmark Hall of Fame, was actually a successful show, one of the most successful of all syndicated game shows.

But "Circle" was having a problem—it seemed to have peaked. Ratings while still very high were not reflecting "all that demographic and psychographic shit they worry about so much" (in the words of Phil Annis) and as a result the show went in search of a gimmick, which turned out to be a "very special two weeks of 'Celebrity Circle,'" a cruise aboard the *St. Michael,* "the world's most glamorous ship filled with the world's most glamorous stars—your very favorites from your very favorite shows including a brand-new addition— everybody's very favorite movie critic!" (all this from the publicity handout) and then two paragraphs about Tobin and all the wonderful things he'd done with his life.

The pay wasn't a great deal over scale but for once

Phil was right about it being "important exposure" and for another thing the cruise was in fact a great one, loaded with women, food, sun, and a certain deference paid him because he was after all that most enviable of American entities, a celebrity.

All he had to do was show up to tape nine segments in the jerry-rigged studio on the main deck and the rest of the time he was free to do whatever he could get away with—if he could spare the time from viewing.

Presently, that seemed to consist of helping out a delicious-looking but definitely strange young woman who kept muttering about someone called Aberdeen.

He was very officious, actually. He came in and clipped on the lights and then made a very manly show of not being disturbed at all over the sight of the blood-soaked body.

He knelt down next to it—knowing she was watching him from behind—the way his hero Alan Ladd might have—and said, as if it needed to be said, "Stabbed."

"Yes."

"And you didn't argue?"

"No."

"You were in the bathroom?"

"Yes."

"Just freshening up?"

"A shower. This was going to be very special."

"I see."

"I'd dated football players before and one U.S. senator but never a network star."

"Ah." What sins "dated" hid.

"And so while you were taking a shower, getting ready for—"

"While I was taking a shower, getting ready for—"

"—the killer came in and—"

"—and hid in the closet."

"The closet?"

She nodded to the louvered doors. "There."

"How do you know?"

"Because I saw him. Or her."

"Him or her?"

She described the getup. "It was supposed to look like a he but it could have been a she. You know?"

"You didn't tell me about the closet before."

"I forgot."

"Is there anything else you forgot?"

"You really think they're going to blame me, don't you?"

For the first time, he noticed how vulnerable she looked. Much younger, and sweet in a midwestern way. By now the blood on her hands and arms had caked. She still held them away from her body as if she did not want them at all.

"I just think you need to get your story straight," he said, softly.

"You're really nice."

Standing up, knees cracking, turning his face away from what had been the handsome towheaded body of Ken Norris, he said, "You mean for a critic."

She smiled. "My father never forgave you for the crack you made about John Wayne."

"All I said was that Wayne made the mistake of confusing his politics with his art. He was a very good actor, actually."

"My father said he wanted to punch you."

"Be sure to invite me to your next family reunion."

Then he stared at her a moment. She stood on one side of the body, he on the other. "I have to ask this."

"Oh, God."

"Did you kill him?"

And she began instantly to cry, soft midwestern-girl tears, and all her lusciousness trembled beneath her white terry-cloth robe and he found himself feeling like a shit again.

"I had to ask."

She kept crying. "I know."

"Do you need some Kleenex?"

"Please."

So he went and got her some Kleenex from the bathroom, which still smelled of steam and perfume, and brought her back a pink handful and said, "Now I'll have to call the captain."

"Will you stay here with me?"

"Yes."

"I really didn't kill him."

"I know."

"I was going to write Aberdeen all about it."

"Who's Aberdeen?"

"A woman at the insurance company."

"Ah."

"But now I don't even care about that."

She stared down at the body of Ken Norris. "He said he'd just finished a pilot and would probably be on CBS next season."

Tobin tried hard not to frown. What a seducer's ploy that had been. "Probably be on CBS next season." He could hear the deep-voiced Norris saying exactly that, that line of lines uttered by thousands of TV has-beens daily to wives, children, creditors, eager midwestern girls, and themselves. Most especially—and desperately—to themselves.

Tobin went and called the captain.

6

"And you believe her?"

"Yes," Tobin said.

"You hesitated a moment."

Tobin shrugged. "You asked me an absolute question that required an absolute answer." He nodded back to the room where Ken Norris's body lay, and where Cindy sat with a dour steward. Tobin smiled. "Absolute answers take a little longer."

"She's very nice-looking."

"Believe it or not, Captain," Tobin said, knowing what the large, white-haired man in the perfectly tailored white uniform was implying, "I've been around nice-looking women before."

They leaned against the railing and watched the silver sea sprawl in the moonlight. The night noises had largely subsided—most people were drunk and passed out, fornicating, or simply sleeping. Tobin watched the horizon line. Easy to imagine that the entire planet was water. That this was a little world unto itself, that there was no other world at all.

"Perhaps he tried something on her and she didn't like it. It could always be self-defense."

"You want an answer right away," Tobin said, "and I understand that. You want to greet your passengers in the morning with the news that, yes, there has been a murder but no, the murderer is not at large. In fact, she's in custody and everything is wonderful."

"I don't want panic. I don't want the cruise ruined."

Tobin said, angrily, "I don't want to see a woman charged with something she didn't do."

"Then you really believe somebody was in the closet?"

"If she says so."

"Then who would it have been?" The captain caught himself and laughed. "I guess that would fall under the general heading of stupid questions, wouldn't it? If we knew who was in the closet, then we'd know the killer."

"Not necessarily."

"What?"

"She didn't say this person was the killer. She just said he or she was in the closet."

"What's the difference?"

Tobin, dragging on his cigarillo and thinking that it wasn't really smoking if you didn't inhale, said, "I'd say there's a good chance that that's the killer—the person in the closet—but we don't know that for sure."

"Then what else would he or she have been doing in the closet?"

"I don't know."

Capt. Robert Hackett, who had the outsize, handsome features of a Roman senator, said, "You really think she's innocent?"

"You talked to her. Do you really think she killed him?"

"Yes."

"God, really?"

"Who else would have done it?"

"The person in the closet."

The captain shook his head. "You really believe there was somebody in the closet?" Before Tobin could respond, Hackett said, "I'd better go tell the other cast members what's going on. There are three of them in the lounge."

Tobin said, "Do you mind if I go with you?"

"No." Then he nodded to the room. "Maybe you'd want to take the young lady for a stroll along the deck while we remove the body. Then we can go down to the lounge. You might tell her we'll get her a different room for the rest of the voyage."

He started back toward the cabin and then paused. "I still think she did it, Mr. Tobin. I don't believe a word about the person in the closet. Not a word."

7   12:54 A.M.

The small lounge was got up art deco, with a smoky, neon ambience long on mirrors, shadows, and black-and-white floor paneling. On the small dance floor a couple in matching Hawaiian shirts performed something fat and slow and melancholy, something very middle-aged that both stunned and saddened Tobin. It was not so much a dance as some simple but profound animal reassurance that if all else failed, they at least had each other. To the right of the bar was a small section of pink love seats and overstuffed chairs and tables of glass and chrome. Behind this was the bar where a thin man in a severe black dinner jacket from the thirties wiped drinking glasses as if he were doing something far beneath his dignity. His glowering gaze grew only more hostile when he saw Tobin and Captain Hackett.

The party, such as it was, lay in the area of the love seats, where three members of "Celebrity Circuit" sat luxuriating in the adoration of some very drunk passengers.

The three members were Kevin Anderson, the blond All-American sort whose canceled series had been "Night Patrol," about an undercover cop; next to him was Susan Richards, a true dark beauty whose canceled series had been "Galloway House," a nighttime soap opera about a very wealthy Irish family; and Todd Ames, the smooth, gray-haired character actor (invariably he played the handsome cad, a more virile George Sanders) whose canceled series had been "Killer's Call," about a professional killer who stalked other professional killers.

Six of their seven fans were about the sort you expected to find—decent enough people, Tobin supposed, from Des Moines or Baltimore or Spokane, stocks and bond people, or retail people, or medical people—but caught up in a very silly moment, that of treating has-been Hollywood types as if they were something special, as if they were golden people not plagued by age or illness or failed relationships or poverty. And maybe that's what it was all about, anyway— maybe that's what people from Des Moines or Baltimore or Spokane *wanted* to believe, that out there in Hollywood was this different, better species, one safe from the sag of jowl, the loss of money, the specter of surgery. Maybe it was somehow comforting to believe in this species.

There was a couple, a husband and wife; two men who wore a few hundred pounds of gold chains around their necks; and two very young and very drunk girls who seemed to be serving as snacks for the two men with the great tonnage of gold chains.

Only one man seemed unimpressed with the three stars. He sat a bit to the left, sipping at a beer not from a long slender glass but directly from the bottle. There was a certain quiet defiance in the gesture but then there was a quiet defiance about the man, period. He wore a sedate western suit—no spangles or piping—a Stetson that sat parked on what was obviously a black toupee, and a gigantic wedding ring. He watched. He listened. He didn't smile and he didn't talk. He did only those two things. He watched. He listened. Captain Hackett and Tobin pushed past him to the three stars.

"Look," said one of the very young girls. "It's that film guy!"

"Tobin!" said her friend.

Husband poked wife and wife poked husband. "It's Tobin," whispered wife.

"The film guy," whispered husband.

Captain Hackett said to the three stars, "I wondered if we might talk with you."

"What's up?" Kevin Anderson grinned drunkenly. "Did Tobin lose his temper and throw somebody overboard?"

Tobin wanted to make an obscene gesture but decided that would only underscore Anderson's point. Tobin was tired of True Temper Tales. He had long ago quit throwing tantrums. For the most part, anyway.

"I'm afraid this is more serious than that," Captain Hackett said.

"Aw, come on," one of the chain-encumbered men said. "Todd was going to tell us which of the 'The Pendergasts' guys is a fag."

"Yeah, which one?" said his buddy.

The captain turned to the fans and said, with the expansive courtliness of one long accustomed to appeasing those he considers beneath him, "I know what an inconvenience this is—getting people like this dragged away from you. But I'll tell you what. If you'll let me have them for just ten minutes . . ." And here he made a gesture the pope would have envied, a sweeping kind of thing that bestowed freedom on these people. "Then if they'd like to come back and spend some more time here in the lounge, the drinks will be on me. How's that?"

"Ten minutes and no more?" asked the eager husband.

"And no more," promised the captain.

Then he indicated to the three confused-looking stars a private party room at the end of the lounge. He quietly asked a steward who had been helping the bartender to go get two other passengers.

"It's that red-haired guy, isn't it?" one of the hairy, golden-chained men called out as the group started to the party room. "He's the fag, isn't he?"

Nothing looks lonelier than a room meant for festivity when nothing festive is going on.

The party room was long and narrow, with beautifully flocked red wallpaper, a dry bar along the west wall, a sensational view of the moon-tipped ocean, and a jukebox, Tobin noted, loaded with as diverse a play list as any forty-year-old drunk could hope for—Sam the Sham & The Pharaohs, Dan Fogelberg, Judy Collins, Firefall, David Bowie, Jackson Browne, Hank Williams (the real one, not the fat-ass no-talent bully boy son living off the old man's rep), Madonna, Michael Jackson, and Patti Page.

The captain, still in the grand style, saw that his guests had the drinks they chose. Tobin had a diet 7-Up.

"Something terrible happened, didn't it?" Susan Richards said. Though she invariably played the beautiful bad woman, off-camera she was often overwrought, her looks somewhat wasted on her unspoken anxieties. She sighed and sounded sorry for herself. "I thought getting out of LA was going to make me feel better. And now this."

Todd Ames slid an arm around her. "We don't know

what happened yet, Susan. Maybe it's not as bad as it would seem. No sense borrowing trouble." As he spoke, he took note of his sleek, gray-haired good looks in the window.

Kevin Anderson said to the captain, "This is really bullshit."

"What is?" the captain said calmly.

"Keeping us all on edge like this."

"I'd simply prefer not to go through it twice," the captain said mildly.

"Something's really wrong," Susan said, touching her breast. "I can feel it."

Anderson stared directly at the captain and said, "Nothing more than heartburn, Susan. It's the food we eat."

The captain looked over at Tobin. He smiled apologetically at Tobin, as if the three stars were the captain's children and they were misbehaving and embarrassing both themselves and him.

Tobin had to find a bathroom. He said, "I'll be back in a minute."

The captain glanced at his watch. "I'd like you all here if you don't mind."

"Just need a bathroom."

"Oh."

"A minute."

"Fine."

Susan said, "Tobin, I thought you and I were friends. You're really going to leave this room and not tell us what's going on?"

"I can't, Susan. At sea the captain is boss."

"What a brownnose," Anderson said in his best blond TV hero way.

Tobin laughed. This was like being in sixth grade. Brownnose. Right. (His all-time favorite line was from

André Malraux, in which an elderly Italian priest is asked if he learned anything hearing confessions for sixty years. The priest thinks for a moment and says, "Yes. There is no such thing as an adult." And fortyish Anderson had just proved the priest's point—as Tobin proved it every day, putting his own age of maturity at eighteen, tops.)

The deal was he just needed to go to the bathroom located at the east end of the lounge and get right back. It was not supposed to be a significant trip.

But as he opened the party room door from inside, he heard the sound of something heavy moving quickly away.

When he looked out, he saw the chunky man in the western suit and the Stetson hurrying back toward the bar. He remembered how intently the man had watched and listened to the celebrities holding court.

He'd been listening again, only this time by leaning against the door.

Tobin wondered more than ever who he was, and what he was doing.

The men's room reminded him of a column he'd written for his college paper in his senior year, all about why men's rooms should have rubber floors that could be easily hosed off.

Presently, the three urinals were occupied by three drunks carrying on an enthusiastic but totally meaningless conversation while paying not the slightest attention to where they aimed.

Tobin took a stall, kicked the lid up with the toe of his shoe, and acted like a very responsible citizen, aiming, and aiming to please.

He left the men's room feeling like a very responsible citizen. Perhaps he'd get a gold star in urine.

8

Tobin had learned that the news of unexpected death is generally greeted in one of two ways—angry denial ("There has to be some mistake") or instant shock, usually expressed by tears or a kind of animal keening that has nothing to do with gender, the ageless noise of grief over the fact that human beings must die.

When he returned to the party room he found two additional guests, "Celebrity Circle"'s producer, Jere Farris, and Cassie McDowell, the thirtyish blond who had played the cute and sweet Ms. Franklin on the recently canceled "McKinley High, USA."

As Tobin reached the dry bar, lighted another cigarillo, and poured himself another glass of diet 7-Up from a big green plastic job that seemed to weigh about eight pounds, Captain Hackett, obviously wanting to break the news in the most efficient manner possible, said, "I'm afraid that Ken Norris was murdered earlier tonight."

Tobin, leaning against the bar, sipping 7-Up and smoking his cigarillo, watched and listened to the various reactions.

Jere Farris, looking almost bankerish in his blue button-down shirt, dark blue slacks, brown belt, penny loafers, and somewhat bookish face, said, "He likes playing practical jokes. Once he got us all up to his hotel room by making us all believe he was going to jump out the window."

Cassie McDowell said, quietly, "The captain isn't fooling, Jere." She brushed a graceful hand back through her bangs. The hand was twitching.

Susan Richards said, bitterly, and apparently to Todd Ames (as if Ken Norris's death were his fault), "I *told* you this was going to be bad news."

"You're sure this isn't some kind of hoax?" Farris said.

Captain Hackett shook his head. "It's no hoax."

"But who would have done it?" Kevin Anderson said.

Tobin watched each of them carefully and then said, pushing away from the dry bar, "The captain is under the impression that a woman named Cindy McBain did it."

"Who the hell is Cindy McBain?" Todd Ames said. "Has she been on television?"

Tobin shook his head. "Another one of Ken's conquests. Or near-conquests. She insists she was taking a shower for their night of bliss. Then she came out and found the lights out in her cabin and Ken dead on her floor."

"Poor Ken," Susan Richards said.

Farris said, "What do you think of her story, Captain, this McBain woman?"

"I don't believe it."

"You think she killed him?"

"Yes." He nodded to Tobin. "She told Mr. Tobin here that she saw somebody hiding in her closet."

"And you believed that, Tobin?" Anderson said. He was getting back into his TV cop role, scorn in his voice.

Tobin had some of his cigarillo. "She might have

done it. But it wouldn't make a lot of sense. Why would she kill him?"

Just then Susan Richards started sobbing, her dark hair swinging across her face, her lovely blue eyes vanished now. Ames took her to him and held her very tightly. Tobin noticed that Ames once again looked at his reflection in the window. Ultimately everything was a role and you had to worry about camera angles, even when you were comforting the grief-stricken.

"I want to get good and drunk," Anderson said. Now he was a beer commercial cowboy. There was a swagger in his voice.

There were times when Tobin wanted to take all the actors in the world, put them on an elevator on the ninetieth floor, then cut the cords. All the way down they'd be worrying about how they looked—appropriately frightened? Appealingly dismayed? At least on "Celebrity Handyman" all the nonacting host worried about was whether he pounded nails with the proper end of the hammer.

"This is just crazy," Cassie McDowell said. "It's unreal." She looked at Tobin. At a post-launch party, something like electricity (of a low-voltage type) had passed between them over the lunch-dinner of duck and champagne, and ever since she'd offered him this kind of twitchy eye contact that could easily be confused with nearsightedness. "Don't you think, Tobin?"

He shrugged, sighed. She startled him by coming over to him and sliding her arms around him and then without warning breaking into tears. She leaked through his sport jacket and his shirt to the flesh of his shoulders. Her tears were warm and inexplicably erotic. He wished his feelings were more appropriate to the moment—the game-show host had, after all, been a fellow human being. He tried hard to form an image of the dead man in his mind and feel some sort of sorrow. But he hadn't liked Ken Norris very much. Their first day shooting Norris had made innumerable on-camera jokes about Tobin's height and then he'd bullied a cameraman till the man had tears in his eyes and then he'd turned his scorn on an effeminate makeup man and then he'd complained aloud, in front of the entire cast, that Susan Richards was drinking again.

"He was no angel, I'll give you that," Susan Richards said now, her tears ceasing. "But he was a damn good host. He really was."

Yes, Tobin thought, he had the looks and demeanor for it. The predatory gaze, the glibness that was almost decadent in its emptiness.

In Tobin's arms, Cassie was calling a halt to her tears too. Apparently tears were doled out in three-minute segments. Like a camera take.

"I'll never forget that Christmas special he did with the handicapped kids," Cassie said, drawing away from Tobin. He realized then why he liked her so much. She was maybe five-two. "He looked so—sincere—when he held those kids on his lap and sang Christmas songs. Even if he did get mad when that kid wet his pants right on Ken's lap." There was a loneliness in her laughter that made Tobin like her even more.

Farris said, "He had a few faults but I'll tell you, he wasn't nearly as cruel as the press said he was. I think they were very unfair to him."

Ames said, "Absolutely. When he dumped his second wife, he had no idea she'd have a stroke a few days later. Yet the press blamed him entirely."

"He wasn't perfect," Susan said again, snuffling. "But he really was a very good host. He really was."

Tobin now watched the captain. Real amusement

played in the older man's eyes. The same kind of amusement Tobin felt.

The captain said to Farris, "Will there be a taping tomorrow?"

"God, there'll have to be. We've got so much money at stake here in the crew and equipment. There'll have to be."

"Then who'll be host?" Cassie said. Apparently the formal mourning period was over. Talk, infinitely more passionate, had turned to career.

Farris, who gave every evidence that he too was about to break down, but from anxiety more than sorrow, ran slender fingers through thinning hair and said, "I'll have to let you know in the morning. We can pick up an additional celebrity panelist by using your wife, Todd, if that's all right?"

Todd Ames's wife was the actress Beth Cross, whose canceled series had been "Crime Town."

"She'd be delighted," Ames said, sounding much happier than he should have under the circumstances. He corrected himself at once, drawing himself erect, getting a glimpse of his gray head in the window once more. "I mean, under these unfortunate conditions."

The captain said, "Well, I will continue to question Miss McBain about this evening and meanwhile, I invite you to stay here and have a few more drinks if you wish."

"Poor Ken," Susan said.

"He really wasn't nearly the jerk people thought," Anderson said. Then he smiled manfully. "I always knew it would be a babe who did him in. That old stud sure did get around."

"I think," Cassie said, using one of the lines from "McKinley High, USA"—with which she'd become inextricably associated—"I think all he needed was some good old-fashioned love."

Tobin had seen that promo at least 4,629 times, where Cassie in a clip faced the camera in close-up and said in her squeaky-clean voice, "I think all he needed was some good old-fashioned love." He'd always wanted to barf.

Nobody should be that treacly. Nobody.

9 1:47 A.M.

"I hope my friends can find a few nicer things to say about me when my time comes," Captain Hackett said as he and Tobin walked along the deck back to Tobin's cabin.

"You noticed that, huh?"

"He wasn't nearly as much of a jerk as most people thought."

"Sure he dumped his wife but how could that possibly help her have a stroke?"

The captain said, "I don't suppose he did much worse to that little handicapped boy who wet his pants than slap him a time or two." He pawed at a chin in need of a shave. "Was he really that much of a jerk?"

"You're asking the wrong guy."

"Why?"

"Because he was unpleasant to me. He let it be known that he considered me a very weak guest panelist and he treated me accordingly. Plus he made jokes about my height."

"Oh, yes. They call you 'Yosemite Sam.' I think my wife told me that."

"I love that name."

"Are you serious?"

"What do you think?"

They walked on a bit. The night was beautiful, the ocean endless, the thrum of powerful engines reassuring evidence of man's illusory dominance over the ocean.

"You don't think she did it, do you?"

"No," Tobin said. "And based on how everybody reacted tonight—Sure he was a wife-beating, child-molesting, embezzling sonofabitch but deep down all he needed was old-fashioned love—I'd say there are at least several other equally good suspects."

"Meaning what?"

"Meaning that if we look beneath the surface, we'll probably find all sorts of reasons he was killed—by one of them."

Captain Hackett sighed. "It just wouldn't make sense that she didn't kill him."

"Of course it would. She'd be the perfect setup."

They reached Tobin's cabin. "They really didn't seem to be very moved by his death, did they?"

Tobin smiled. "I remember back in 1953, when I was very young. I was over at a friend's house watching TV—they were the only people on the block with a set—and news came that Stalin had died. They interrupted 'Mr. Peepers.' I've never forgotten it. Everybody was euphoric because Stalin had died. It seemed as if everything in the world was going to be all right." He nodded back toward the lounge. "I kind of had that same sense tonight, didn't you?"

"Nothing you could prove," the captain said.

Tobin said, "Not yet, anyway."

10

In the dream he sat in a vast dark movie theater and on the screen was *Invasion of the Body Snatchers* and Dana Wynter, whom he still thought the most beautiful actress of her time, was just about to fall asleep and in so doing become one of the pod people and he was in seventh grade again and watching the movie in the State Theater and held spellbound not only by the beautiful noir writing and directing but mostly there was just Dana Wynter, the luxuriant elegance of that face, the silken dark hair and silken dark gaze, domestic and exotic in equal parts—and now, as always in the dream, he cried out for her to not close her eyes, not to become one of the pod people, cried out to no avail . . .

Knocking woke him.

Disoriented, he had to put his circumstances together one word at a time.

Ship.

Cabin.

Sleep.

Dream.

Knock.

Door.

"Huh?" he said, peering through the safety chain.

She wore her white terry-cloth robe again. Her hair looked a bit mussed. Her wonderful mouth looked forlorn.

"They gave me a new cabin," she said. Moonglow made a nimbus of her blond hair.

"Yes."

"But I couldn't sleep."

"Ah."

"I tried."

"Umm."

"But I couldn't."

"Uh."

"You're not awake, are you?"

"Mhrmw."

"What?"

He shrugged.

"I'm sorry," she said.

He shrugged again.

"I shouldn't have bothered you. I'm just lonely and afraid. Not even telling Aberdeen everything helped. Well, not 'telling her.' Writing her, actually. I mean, I put everything down. Everything he said to me—you know about that really annoying guy—and everything I said to him. I had quite a bit of champagne and even told him about that United pilot and what we did in the bathroom that time. And then how he was stabbed and all and . . ."

By now he was sufficiently awake that he could say, "Do you want to come in?"

"Do you ever sleep with women?"

"As often as I can."

"I'm serious, Mr. Tobin."

"Please don't call me Mr." He wondered if his dreaded sleep-breath (which the army could use as the ultimate weapon) was wafting in her direction. "It makes me feel even older than I am."

"I'm sorry."

"It's all right."

"But do you?"

"Sleep with women?"

"Yes."

"As in sharing a bed with rather than making love?"

"Yes, on occasion when I've been heartbroken or especially lonely, women have been nice enough to do that for me, and on occasion I've been nice enough to do that for women in similar circumstances."

"I need to be held."

"All right."

"Very tightly."

"All right."

"I need to be a little girl again."

"All right."

"But I really don't want to be touched. Not sexually."

"All right."

"Really?"

"Really."

"It's a lot to ask."

He leaned over and kissed her, nuclear breath or not, on the forehead. Chastely. The way he did his daughter when she was but a year and sleeping with her fuzzy pink bear.

Her body was more wondrously curved than he'd even imagined and at first there in the dark, her lying against him, the water and the moonlight inviting immemorial urges, it had been difficult indeed but then she'd begun to cry, so softly he'd been moved far more than he would have thought possible, and then he had a frank and a sharp discussion with his penis about decorum and appropriateness and giving-Cindy-my-word, and finally then, next to her sweet scent and sweeter warmth, he fell asleep.

11

Tobin had once read a rather long and surprisingly fascinating book on medieval theater and how, when the theater wagons pulled into the small towns surrounding London or Rome or Prague, the townspeople would come forth with gifts of flowers and food.

What audiences these days had to offer was not much different, really. But their gifts were the special attention they lavished on people who were essentially nobodies, has-been's or would-be's (Tobin always put himself in the latter category), and instead of flowers their mouths bloomed with laughter over the trite jokes of mid-level celebrity. Game show or melodrama, they searched for some respite from the grind of work or dull relationships or any number of fears.

And that was why there were so many of them this morning, the ocean sky cloudless blue, the ocean calm and unending green, on the brilliant white deck, where the episodes of "Celebrity Circle" were taped.

Jere Farris, the producer, tense under the best conditions, looked even tenser and more exhausted this morning as he tore himself this way and tore himself that way to address all sorts of problems—from lighting to sound checks to makeup to cue cards to the routine the warm-up comedian was going to use.

Tobin was in his seat behind the big horseshoe-shaped panel. He had a nameplate in front of him, a guide for all the millions of folks at home who might not have a clue as to who he was. He wore a Hawaiian shirt—even though they weren't anywhere near Hawaii. As Farris said, "It's tropical, that's all that matters to Mr. and Mrs. Midwest, it's tropical."

Everybody on the panel wore Hawaiian shirts and leis, and had gigantic fruit drinks in front of them, and redwood-sized plastic palm trees behind them so that the picture that went home was of this fantastic floating paradise, complete with insert shots of truly incredible babes lolling about the swimming pool and snapshot-like inserts of the various celebrities doing "tropical" stuff: Tobin playing deck tennis, looking short next to the gorgeous Susan Richards; macho ex-TV cop Kevin Anderson pumping iron as two women with a lot of suntan goop on, so they'd look darker, standing to his right supposedly playing the ukuleles they hugged to their great bikinied bosoms; and Cassie McDowell leading a group of "young-at-heart older citizens" in a chorus of "God Bless America."

It was ducky, it was plucky, it was yucky and Tobin, in his stupid screaming shirt, was right in the middle of it.

The warm-up comedian, Marty Gerber, was one of those rare young comedians who didn't use shock material for his laughs, favoring instead almost gentle comments on the perverse nature of human beings, some of the most perverse of whom were the gaudy tourists in their gaudy clothes spread now like a lurid flower garden over the deck where the show was being taped.

As Marty skillfully worked the audience, the rest of the crew went through the final breakdown of lighting, camera positioning, and sound checks.

"We've got three segments to tape today! Three segments!" Jere Farris said, clapping his hands at a lighting man whom he'd perceived dawdling. "Do you understand how much money we're losing?"

Farris, tart, given to matronly hand-clapping and a certain prissiness in expression, was never a favorite with crews, most of whom ran to overweight, blue-jeaned guys who hated anybody who was on camera, but hated especially people in position to give them orders. Especially guys who gave orders by clapping hands.

Tobin ducked down and made an elaborate pretense of tying his penny loafer. At least he hoped that people had the impression he was tying his shoe. What he was really doing, of course, was pouring pure silver vodka from his pure silver flask—which was mounted by Velcro backing to his sock—into his stupid pink-yellow fruit drink.

As he poured, he took the opportunity to admire Cassie McDowell's perfect ankles.

Then he sat back up and began sipping with quiet satisfaction.

He had just sort of wiggled himself back into position when he noticed the makeup woman, a very shy, graceful, twentyish girl named Joanna Howard, staring at him. If Tobin were ever asked to cast a film about the Amish, he'd choose her—she had that kind of severe prettiness that sometimes is far more interesting than any other sort, perhaps because it's touched with mystery. Joanna rarely spoke but only nodded, rarely smiled but only sort of inclined her head when she realized that she was supposed to laugh but could not, apparently, find the appropriate sound. Then there were her clothes. Though the cruise was "tropical," she always wore heavy white silk blouses that came all the way down to her wrists and very heavy designer jeans and heavy woolen argyle socks and white tennis shoes of the Keds variety. Her blue gaze fascinated him, and he wondered now how long she'd been standing there and if she'd guessed what he'd just done.

"Did you see that?"

She looked puzzled.

"No, I guess you didn't."

"Your nose," she said.

"My nose?"

"Needs powder."

"Oh."

"Shiny."

"Ah."

So she did his nose to reduce the glare and then she did his cheeks and jaw again, apparently just as a precaution.

As she worked, he said, "Do you ever relax?"

He saw her cheeks color.

"I didn't mean to embarrass you, Joanna. And I wasn't flirting." You had to treat her like a very skittish animal. "I just mean, are you having fun on the trip?"

She nodded. "Sure."

"Why don't I ever see you in any of the lounges?"

"Oh. This allergy, I guess."

"Allergy."

"To alcohol."

"Oh."

"But I brought some good books."

"Oh."

For the first time ever, he saw her smile. "Books are better than people sometimes."

"True enough."

"I'm reading Thomas Wolfe."

And she was of course at just the right age for Wolfe. Only later on—after your first kid, your first firing, and the death of a parent—did you realize that Wolfe's concerns were those of a very talented but very self-consumed fourteen-year-old.

"You don't like him?"

"Why do you say that?" Tobin asked.

"You just made a face."

"Oh. Well, I'd have to say he's not my favorite."

"Who's your favorite?"

"Oh, gosh."

"I guess that was a kind of stupid question, huh?"

Seeing that he'd embarrassed her, he put a hand out to touch her forearm, but before his fingers could quite reach her, she jerked her arm away.

He said, "Graham Greene."

"What?"

She was still looking upset over the fact that he'd tried to touch her.

"If you pressed me about my very favorite writer," Tobin said, "I'd have to say Graham Greene." He was staring at the space where her arm had been. The arm she wouldn't let him touch. "I . . . I'm sorry, Joanna. I didn't mean anything by that."

Half-whispering, she said, "I know." Then, "Well, I'd better get back to Fritz and see if he needs help." Fritz was the head makeup person. Then she paused and seemed to gather her strength and said, "You know what?"

"What?"

"I don't like Graham Greene any better than you like Thomas Wolfe."

He sensed how heroic it was for a girl so shy to say something like this and he broke into an exultant grin, happy for her.

His hand started out automatically to touch her—he was that sort, a toucher, which some people liked and some definitely did not—but she was gone before he could commit another mistake.

He hoisted his fruit drink and looked around him, at the oval of audience in front, at the scurrying technicians all about.

Marty was just now getting the audience to really howl.

Jere Farris—dashing about, sweaty and hysterical—clapped his hands at everybody in his way, as if he were a farmer scattering chickens.

Plump people from Cleveland whistled as the ersatz hula girls entered stage right.

Two cameramen knocked over a light as they pulled their camera to the right. The sound was sharp as a gunshot. Some laughed, some screamed.

The show itself was nothing much at all.

Inside a semicircle of celebrities (technically, the thing should have been called "Celebrity SemiCircle") sat three contestants, each of whom was handed a card with one-half of an answer (such as "E="), and they then had two chances to choose the celebrity with the other half of the answer ("D Cup" would be a typical "naughty" celebrity response, sure to drive Dubuque crazy).

The contestants, of course, had all been prescreened to prove that they were pneumatic grinners-laughers-jumpers-up-and-down, that subspecies of humanity endemic to TV shows where ordinary folks can win cold Yankee cash.

The surprise of the day—and a long, grinding day it was—was Todd Ames's smooth performance as host. With his theatrically handsome features, his sleek gray hair, his almost courtly manner and his apparently genuine intelligence, he was in fact much better than the somewhat combative Ken Norris had been. Norris, famous for his occasionally too-tart responses, had always conveyed a kind of Malibu contempt for the masses, as if he might catch something from standing next to them. But Ames showed evidence of the sort of vaguely condescending paternalism that Americans love so much in their ministers, politicians, and doctors.

Halfway through the second show, Tobin began to wonder if, in fact, Ames had been rehearsing for just this moment—he seemed so composed, so ready for the task you had the eerie feeling that . . .

But would one actor kill another merely to ascend to the star position of the most popular game show in TV syndication?

Are you crazy?

Halfway through the third segment a chopper appeared against the blue sky and hovered above the opposite end of the gigantic cruise ship.

A rope mechanism was lowered and a pulley system put into action. A long, lumpy black bag was borne upward into the chopper's belly as the air was torn furiously by the whirling blades and the white-uniformed stewards held their hats in place from the wind.

Do not ask for whom the pulley pulls.

The cruise ship was off-loading the body of former "High Rise" star and TV game-show host Ken Norris.

It would taint cruise ship fun to have a rotting stiff down in the meat lockers. Your steak just wouldn't taste the same.

12

3:17 P.M.

After the taping, Tobin went back to his cabin, took a shower, changed into a plain blue button-down shirt, stuck a cigarillo in his teeth, and then went in search of the captain's number-one suspect, Cindy McBain.

At this time of day, the ship was alive with a dizzying variety of activity. People jogged, participated in aerobics classes, played deck games, sat around one of the three swimming pools, sat in lounges listening to puppy-eager performers, did really dumb numbers like trying to shimmy underneath limbo poles while friends sat around and drunkenly laughed, and generally milled about on the various decks trying to have the sort of fun the brochure not only suggested but vaguely demanded you have.

He went past a barber shop, a beauty parlor, a hospital, a foursome of elevators; he went past a golf-driving range, a trapshooting area, a library, a discotheque. Finally, he tried the casino, where the noise and energy of gambling were almost vulgar on the otherwise lazy air, and there he found her.

She was at a blackjack table and she was sitting with Cassie McDowell and watching the dealer, a swarthy man in a white shirt with epaulets that would have delighted Rudyard Kipling, dispatch cards face-up, face-down with dizzying precision.

"Hi, Cindy," he said when he reached her.

She was concentrating on her cards so that when she glanced up, her blue eyes didn't focus for a moment and she resembled an infant coming awake.

"Oh. Hello."

"I'm trying to cheer her up," Cassie said, pointing to the drinks in front of them. Clear, they were presumably vodka and tonics. Cassie flicked her eyes indicating she wasn't getting the job done very well. Today Cassie wore a white lacy blouse and dark blue slacks. She resembled a very lovely grade-schoolteacher from Elgin, Illinois.

Cindy, contrarily, was overdressed, in a black gownlike frock with a scoop neck that no doubt made men happy and women uneasy. Cindy said, "I burst?"

"Bust." The dealer sighed. "Bust is the word. Not burst." Obviously he'd explained this to her many times. Obviously he was tired of it. "And," he said, flipping over her card, "yes, you did. You've got twenty-four."

"Darn," Cindy said. The way she leaned, you might have thought she'd fall off her stool.

Tobin moved closer to her, let her lean against him. It was not an unpleasant duty at all.

"I was never any good at blackjack, either," Tobin said.

"How much have I lost?" Cindy asked the dealer gravely.

"Eighty dollars, miss," the dealer said.

"Gosh," Cindy said, marveling. "Nearly a day's pay."

The dealer made a little clucking sound.

Tobin glanced around the casino. The cruise ship folks had done their best to turn it into a mini–Las Vegas—with a wall of slot machines, a baccarat table, poker tables, squirrel cages, and enough green felt to cover the floor of the Astrodome. Even in the afternoon the place smelled of cigarette smoke and whiskey and affected the sort of artificial darkness Tobin associated with forlorn midday drinking sessions—of which he'd had more than his share lately.

"Why don't we go for a walk?"

"Where?" Cindy said.

"Around the boat. Lovely afternoon."

Then he wondered why Cassie would look so sour about his proposal. Did she simply resent being left out?

Cindy turned to Cassie. "Maybe that's a good idea. We can finish talking about—well, you know—later on. OK?"

Cassie flushed. Even in the shadows of the casino, Tobin could see how upset she looked, uncomfortable that Cindy had raised the subject of their conversation.

"Just go on," Cassie said hurriedly. "Have a good time."

But her gaze flashed with anger, and it was for Tobin.

In a voice that viewers of "McKinley High, USA" would have been shocked to hear, the demure Cassie McDowell snapped her fingers at a passing waiter and said, "Get me another vodka tonic. And put some goddamn vodka in it this time, all right?"

The waiter nodded and left.

"Gosh, Cassie sure seemed crabby right at the last there."

"Didn't she though."

"She's real nice."

"Yes, she is."

"You'd never guess she was a TV star and I was a secretary at an insurance company."

"Some of us biggies are like that."

"You're being sarcastic."

"You just make too big a fuss over celebrities is all. They're not much different from anybody else—a little more insecure maybe."

"I notice you said 'they're.' Aren't you a celebrity?"

"I suppose."

"You don't sound very happy about it."

"I started off writing for a newspaper. I had an old Dodge then and a wife I loved a great deal and two very wonderful children and someday I was going to write a novel and I'll be damned if I can figure out why I let it all go."

"Gosh, I don't know why you would either."

"But I did."

"Another woman?"

"A series of them."

"Oh."

"You don't sound impressed."

"I just have a thing about married men who play around."

"I know. Adultery's always ugly, no matter how fashionable it becomes."

"That isn't what I meant. I mean, I wish I could sound noble about it but it's just that I went out with two different married men and fell in love with them both and they both strung me along."

"Oh."

"But I don't like adultery much, anyway. If I ever get married I'm going to try very hard to stay faithful."

"It isn't always easy."

"Maybe we've just never been in love."

"Yes," Tobin said. "Yes, maybe it's that simple after all."

By now they had climbed the stairs to the next deck up, where they saw an aerobics class being conducted on the teakwood deck outside the glass-paneled gymnasium.

"How about a 7-Up?" Tobin said, nodding to some outdoor tables near the railing.

"Nothing stronger?"

"I don't think either of us needs it."

"You're not suspected of murder."

"Did the captain say any more to you?"

"Yes, he came around this morning with the ship's doctor. A very cold man named Devane."

By now he'd steered her to a small imitation sidewalk café complete with yellow lawn umbrellas and matching yellow furniture. They faced away from the joggers, which was just as well. Even though the glass afforded Tobin glimpses of lovely women, he did not need to feel guilty about his lack of exercise. There was far too much else to be remorseful over.

He ordered two diet 7-Ups and said, "So what did the captain want?"

"He wanted this Dr. Devane to look at my hands. Isn't that weird?"

"Did he say why?"

"No."

"So he looked at your hands."

"Ummm," she said, sipping the first of her drink.

"And what did he say?"

"He just sort of glanced at the captain and shook his head."

"But he didn't say anything else?"

"No."

"That is odd."

"And scary."

Tobin said, "Maybe not."

"No?"

"No. It sounds to me as if they came there looking for something and didn't find it."

"I didn't kill him."

"I know."

"I'm just a secretary."

"Yes."

"From Kansas City."

He touched her hand. "And a sweet one."

"You're so nice."

"Don't put any nobility on me."

"No?"

"No. This is all probably a protracted attempt at seduction."

She might have been squinting in the late afternoon sunlight but he knew it was a wince instead.

"I used to be sort of promiscuous." She was turning him down.

"We all were."

"I mean, I feel guilty about it."

"So do I. Sometimes, anyway."

"I was even kind of a groupie with certain types of men."

He smiled. "Insurance men?"

She laughed. "No. They're just as dull as they're supposed to be. But you know . . ."

"Jocks, airplane pilots, doctors?"

"Right. All the men I met in singles bars."

"Well, that decade is behind us."

"But I was still pretty much that way until the thing happened with Ken Norris. I mean, I was going to sleep with him and I'd only met him a few hours earlier. I even sort of plotted it."

"You did?"

"Yes. I saw him arguing with Todd Ames, and then

he walked out of the bar to the railing and I pretended to walk out and get lost and just sort of run into him. It was very calculated. I just wanted to be able to tell Aberdeen that on my cruise I'd slept with a TV star."

"I want to know more about his argument with Todd Ames."

Her smooth, carefully tended face showed curiosity. "You think he might have killed Ken?"

Tobin shrugged. "What were they arguing about?"

"I don't know. There was so much noise in the bar I couldn't tell."

"You sure they were arguing?"

"Oh, yes. Ken threw his drink in Todd's face."

"Did Ken say anything about this later, when you were alone?"

"Not exactly. He was pretty drunk, sort of rambling most of the night, but I got the impression he didn't think much of the panelists on the show."

"Why's that?"

"He had something derogatory to say about each of them."

"But did he say anything at all about his argument with Todd Ames?"

"Just one thing and it didn't make much sense. He laughed when I asked him about it and he said 'Todd's just sick of payday.'"

"Payday? He didn't elaborate?"

"Huh-uh." She had some diet 7-Up. He watched her lips. They were wonderful lips, full and rich as a seventeenth-century Italian countess. "But, you know, Tobin, I don't think any of them like each other."

"Any of 'Celebrity Circle?'"

"Right."

"What makes you say that?"

"That's why I'm half-bombed."

"Why?"

"Drinking with Cassie McDowell. She wasn't as blunt as Ken, of course—when we were drinking this afternoon—but any time I'd mention any of the cast, I'd sense this coldness come over her." She gave him a cute little half-frown. "I'm glad secretaries get along better than celebrities." He could see the alcohol begin to fade from her gaze. She had some more 7-Up. "Anyway, she sure asked me a lot of questions."

"About what?"

"If a redheaded woman was following us or anything."

"A redheaded woman?"

"Yes."

"Did she say who the woman was?"

"No."

"Was a redheaded woman following you?"

"Not following us exactly. But I remember coming around the corner of the lounge—I really felt proud of myself, Tobin, being on Ken's arm and all—and there was a middle-aged woman, a nice-looking one with a large beauty mark on her right cheek, standing alone by the deck, smoking a cigarette and just watching us. When we passed her, Ken muttered some kind of name under his breath, and the woman gave him this really . . . arrogant's the only word I can think of . . . this real arrogant smile. Like she knew something really bad about Ken and he knew she knew it."

"But she didn't say anything?"

"No."

"Hmmm. Have you seen her around today?"

"No. But then I haven't been any place really except my cabin and the casino. And the only reason I went there was because Cassie came and got me."

"Oh, she got you?"

≈ 55

"Yes."

"She really wanted some information."

"Yeah, now that I think about it, I guess she did."

Tobin stood up. "How about dinner tonight?"

"You're leaving me?"

"Does that mean yes?"

She smiled her midwestern girl smile and he loved it. "Yes, it means yes, but why are you leaving?"

"I need to see a couple of people."

"Who?"

"The captain for one." Then it was his turn to smile. "And a redheaded woman with a beauty mark on her right cheek."

He walked past the aerobics class, making note of the various expensive aerobic suits and of the bodies inside the suits, and the disco music and the soft, warm ocean breeze made him feel younger and more powerful than he had in a long time.

The captain was in some sort of meeting and would not see him, and bribing four different stewards turned up not a single red-haired woman. "We have six hundred and five cabins, sir. That's a lot of passengers," one steward explained, stuffing Tobin's ten-dollar bill into his pocket.

Tobin went back to his own cabin and fast-forwarded through two videos. He doubted he was missing much with *Biker Girls on Mars* or his least favorite actor, Dustin Hoffman, doing *Hedda Gabler* and playing, à la his famous *Tootsie* turn, Hedda herself.

Finished with these two, Tobin then counted the stack of unseen videos in the corner. Twenty-six more to race through before the cruise ended. Starting inevitably to feel guilty about the short shrift he gave even films such as *Halloween High*, he fortunately saw among the remaining tapes by Val Lewton, John Ford, William Freidkin, Don Seigel, and Ida Lupino—a very good director as well as actress—a few movies he really wanted to see.

But for now, tired, he napped.

He wasn't sure how long he'd been asleep before he heard the screaming just outside his cabin door.

13

5:18 P.M.

Jumping from bed, grabbing his pants and getting into them the way he'd been forced once when an angry husband had been pounding up the stairs, Tobin ran to his door and threw it open.

There, pushed back against the rail, two women struggled over a small brown leather notebook one of them held. Tobin wasn't sure which one owned the thing—all he knew was that the two resembled TV wrestlers, impressive to watch but ineffective.

Tobin, rubbing sleep from his face, walked over to them. Out on the rim of the vast ocean you could see the round yellow sun begin slowly to sink, and closer by a steamer, gray and industrial, chopped through the calm water.

Other passengers had responded to the screams as well and had now tumbled out of their cabins, watching the two women as Tobin approached them.

"Anything wrong?"

It was a silly question and he knew it instantly but he was too sleepy to care.

He pushed himself between the two women and their wrestling ceased.

The dark-haired, slightly pudgy woman he knew, because she was Jere Farris's wife.

Her opponent—a red-haired woman who would have been beautiful if not for a certain hardness in her Katharine Hepburn gaze—he assumed was the one

Cindy McBain had told him about. She had a beauty mark on her right cheek. It was a real beauty mark and a nice one.

The redhead snapped the notebook to her breast, then jammed it quickly into her purse, which she snapped shut with the finality of a bank vault closing for the night.

"You bitch," Alicia Farris said. She was a fortyish woman who knew how to dress for her somewhat hefty size, her clothes running to loose and expensive garments that managed to be both sedate and stylish. She was probably fifty pounds overweight but managed to look only twenty. Her face, with good if broad bones, was beautifully made up and her gray eyes were lovely. Among "Celebrity Circle" members, the joke was that Jere was her male clone, and it was true that she did give the impression of managing him rather than being married to him. But Tobin had had drinks with her a few times and found her bright and funny without being cruel or bitchy, something that could not be said about many show-biz wives who stayed home and sharpened knives while hubby went out and dazzled the masses.

"You mind if I ask what's going on, Alicia?" Tobin said.

"It's this bitch, Iris Graves!"

Iris only smiled, as if she were quite used to being called names.

"Anyway, I'm afraid it isn't your business," Alicia said. Then, more softly, "It really isn't, Tobin." She didn't take her eyes off the redhead.

Then Alicia, conscious suddenly of the other passengers watching her, pushed past Tobin and moved on down the deck, her black high heels sharp against the decking, leaving Tobin standing next to the woman.

Her blessings were bountiful, as her tight white T-shirt and stone-washed jeans revealed. And in addition to her somewhat overwhelming body, which managed to combine the spectacular with the graceful, she had very green eyes and cute little ears bearing giant loops of gold, and teeth so white they had to be capped but weren't. Only the imperiousness of her gaze troubled him. Perhaps, in a previous life, she'd been Benito Mussolini.

She turned to go and Tobin put a hand on her arm.

She glanced at him as if he'd just mooched a quarter. "I don't like being touched," she said.

"What's so important about that notebook?"

"My God, do you really expect me to answer that?" She sounded genuinely shocked.

"And why are you following Cassie McDowell?"

She looked at him and shook her head. "I've watched your show so I know you are stupid, Mr. Tobin. I just didn't know how stupid."

A few of the onlookers laughed at her remark. They also watched admiringly as she walked away.

One sunburned seventy-year-old in red Bermuda shorts and a green short-sleeved shirt said to Tobin, "Are you always that lucky with women?"

Tobin grinned at him. "Only when I bathe regularly."

The man said, "Just watch yourself with that little secretary from Kansas."

Tobin felt his blood chill. "What?"

The man now seemed uneasy. "I just meant . . ."

"You shouldn't have said anything, Ernie," his wife said. She wore a straw hat and what appeared to be knickers and seemed pleasant enough.

"No," Tobin said. "Please let him go on. How do you know about the secretary from Kansas?"

"Well, you know what happened to Ken Norris last night."

"Right. He was killed."

The man shrugged. "Well, the stewards are telling us that the captain thinks she killed him. The secretary."

The sonofabitch, Tobin thought, thinking of the lugubrious captain, a man far more capable of deviousness than Tobin would have given him credit for.

"I didn't mean to upset you," the man said, sounding increasingly defensive.

"That's fine. Didn't mean to startle you."

"Come on, Ernie. Let's go have a mai-tai." The wife smiled at Tobin. "Ernie's always putting his foot in it."

Tobin went back to his cabin and tried to sleep. Uselessly. Instead he kept thinking about the captain, a man whom he'd begun to dislike in a serious way. Finally forcing himself to forget the captain, he started to doze. Then he began worrying about other things, worrying being a process that was with him from the time he opened his eyes till he closed them at the end of the day. There were the children to worry about and his career and his health and there was always the state of his soul, even though he was not sure if he had one. He wanted to be one of those people who could simply put things out of their minds but knew he never would. Ever.

Then he started wondering about the redhead, and why she'd been wrestling with Alicia Farris over a notebook.

Finally, seeing that he'd never get any sleep, he got up, took a shower, dressed for dinner, and went in search of Captain Hackett.

If he couldn't get lucky with any of the women on board, then perhaps he could solve a mystery.

14 6:42 P.M.

"You seem angry, Mr. Tobin."

"You're spreading rumors about Cindy McBain."

"And what rumors would those be, Mr. Tobin?"

"You know damn well what rumors."

"I see."

"And you know damn well why you're spreading them."

"And why would that be, Mr. Tobin?"

"Because if everybody aboard the ship thinks she's the killer, they don't have to worry about the real killer running around loose. That's pretty goddamn despicable, if you ask me."

"The thing is, Mr. Tobin, I don't remember asking you."

Captain Hackett, still looking as if he were about to walk onto a movie set where he would portray a cruise ship captain, indicated a small shelf of bourbons and Canadian whiskeys behind his large oak desk. With the ceiling fan and the louvered blinds and the large bookcase with the sort of leather-bound editions that were never read, there was a certain studied snottiness about the room, capped by the gigantic globe on an easel in the corner, the sort of globe God probably had. "Bourbon?"

"Don't try to change the subject, Captain."

"I hardly think a bourbon would deter you from your appointed rounds, Mr. Tobin. I was simply being polite." For the first time, Tobin felt something positive about Hackett. There was a hint of irony in his tone and Tobin always believed, perhaps wrongly, that irony was a mark of genuine intelligence.

"Then I'll be polite and accept it."

"That's very charitable of you."

The captain poured healthy doses of sipping bourbon into large cut-glass snifters and handed one to Tobin.

Tobin took a sip, enjoyed it much more than he should have, then said, "You found out something this morning, didn't you?"

"Found out?"

"You and a Dr. Devane went to Cindy McBain's cabin. The doctor examined her for something. I got the impression he was disappointed. Which means that your case against Cindy is getting weaker and weaker."

"I wouldn't assume that, Mr. Tobin."

"If you really thought you had something against her, you would have had Cindy taken off the boat with the body and arrested."

The captain took his first sip of whiskey. Purple dusk tinted his white hair in a nimbus of electric blue. His Roman senator features were more imposing than ever. "You've heard of the principle of the greater good, Mr. Tobin."

"Yes. In Philosophy 101."

"Well, Mr. Tobin, sometimes I believe it's an unfortunate principle we must follow."

"In other words, give the passengers peace of mind at Cindy's expense."

Hackett smiled. He appeared both ironic and weary. "People are very emotional, especially in herds."

"Herds?"

"Like it or not, Mr. Tobin, we're animals, and we act

like animals, especially in times of crisis." From a carved wooden humidor on the corner of his desk, he took a cigar, offering Tobin one as he did so.

"I quit a while back."

"Too bad. Cigars are a real pleasure."

"Well, smoking cigars isn't like smoking cigarettes, I suppose."

"Not quite as bad. Certainly not as bad for lung cancer rates. About the same for oral and throat cancer, unfortunately."

"You sure know how to talk a guy into taking a cigar."

"Even in our small pleasures, there is some element of risk, Mr. Tobin." He lifted his glass of bourbon. "The rate of esophagus cancer, for instance, increases with every drink of alcohol we have."

"Remind me to invite you to my next party."

"And it's the same with the principle of the greater good. There is some risk in it, I realize."

"That's nice of you, especially since you don't happen to be a frightened twenty-eight-year-old woman from Kansas City."

"She hardly seems helpless."

"Meaning what?"

"I have daughters of my own, Mr. Tobin. I don't like to think they're the sort who'd go to a man's room on the first night they met him."

"She's not perfect, Captain. That doesn't mean she's a terrible woman."

"Still."

Tobin had more bourbon. "Why did you have the doctor examine her this morning? What were you looking for?"

"Why should you need to know something like that, Mr. Tobin?"

"Because I'm trying to help Cindy."

"I seem to recall that you helped solve the murder of your partner."

"If you're saying I'm not a detective, you're right. But then neither are you." He finished his drink and set it down. "And I'd appreciate knowing why you had the doctor examine her."

"I'm afraid that's classified."

"'Classified' information on a cruise ship?"

Hackett smiled and not unpleasantly. "A holdover from my navy days, I suppose."

Tobin stood up. "You know she didn't do it and I know she didn't do it, and I'd like you to stop spreading those rumors just to cover your own ass."

"Your reputation seems to be true."

"Which reputation? There are several of them."

"That you're something of a hothead, Mr. Tobin."

"I just don't want to see her suffer anymore, Captain. Believe it or not, having somebody stabbed to death in your cabin is a very unnerving experience. She'll never forget it. Her whole life will be divided very neatly in two because of it." He was angry and he jabbed at the air with a small sharp finger. He wasn't tough but he was capable of rage and many times that was far more imposing than being tough. "She's a nice kid and she doesn't deserve to be used as a tranquilizer for the rest of the ship. You understand?"

"I don't like being threatened, Mr. Tobin."

"Right now, I don't give a damn what you like, Captain." He jabbed out the cigar he'd been smoking. "Right now, I don't give a damn at all."

15

What he wanted was a burger and fries (hell, a *cheese*burger and fries) and not the McDonald's kind, either. He wanted the kind you used to go into neighborhood burger joints for, where the guy made them on a grill right in front of you, and maybe even cut an edge out of the patty and said, "That done enough for you," and then you got a bottle of Heinz ketchup and some big chunky sweet dill slices and some wide silver slices of onion and a few dollops of mustard for taste and, man, when you tasted it, you wanted to cry it was so good. So frigging good.

Instead, spread before him tonight under lights more appropriate to lighting a Vegas star, was a vast table filled with stuff called Scallop Brochettes with Lime Butter and Costolette di Agnello and Spinach, Fennel, and Pink Grapefruit Salad. And lots of other dishes equally fancy and equally not burger and french fries.

He ended up conning the waiter into bringing him a tunafish sandwich and some potato chips.

"You're not taking advantage of it," Cindy McBain said. She wore a baby blue sweater and dark blue skirt. The simple pearl necklace reminded him of high school and her chignon gave her an elegance he hadn't noticed before. She still looked tired but she also managed to look dazzled by the spread of exotic food and the carnival atmosphere provided by the third-rate lounge act presently on the stage.

"You sure you don't want a bite of my . . ." Cindy couldn't pronounce what she was eating. "Stuff."

"No, thanks."

"A bite wouldn't kill you."

"This crap, you can't be too sure."

"What's wrong with this . . . crap?"

"Maybe it's just my mood."

"Well, why don't you take just a teensy bite?"

She was like a six-year-old. Gentle but persistent. He was damn well going to have a bite. He was damn well going to be festive.

He pushed his face forward to her, in the wavering candlelight, and put out his tongue.

"You look like you're going to receive communion." Cindy giggled.

"Lay it on me, Father."

Cindy giggled again and started feeding him. He felt like an infant. It wasn't a completely terrible feeling, either. Sometimes being an infant didn't seem to be the worst fate in the world. People fussing over you all the time and playing giggy-goo-goo and wiping your butt for you and suffocating you with love and animal crackers. There were a hell of a lot worse gigs in the world than that one.

He was taking a bite of something that tasted remarkably like Kraft Cheeze-Whiz when, peripherally, he saw the man who'd been listening outside the party room door last night before the captain had told the "Celebrity Circle" about Ken Norris's death.

Tonight he wore another western-style suit, a gray one without frills, and the Stetson, which he took off and set on the table with a certain air of ceremony.

Abruptly, like a man used to being obeyed, he raised his hand and snapped his finger and a waiter, wary at being summoned this way, moved quickly to him. The man gave every impression of being competent, knowing, and more than likely dangerous. Tobin wondered more than ever who he was, and why he'd been listening at the door last night.

"He's interesting, isn't he?" Cindy said.

"Ummm."

"Ken didn't like him."

Tobin brought his attention back to her. "What?"

"Ken didn't like him."

"How do you know?"

"Because we saw him on the veranda, coming back to my cabin."

"And?"

"Ken got very tense."

"You sure?"

"He'd been holding my arm and he really gave it a squeeze. It hurt."

"But he didn't say anything about him?"

"No."

"And you didn't see the man again?"

"Huh-uh. Not till just now." Then she inclined her head back to where the man in the western suit sat. "Hey, look."

Tobin turned just in time to see the red-haired woman who'd been wrestling with Alicia Farris sit down at the man's table.

"The Odd Couple," Cindy said.

"Really."

"But it doesn't seem like romance."

"It doesn't?"

"Look at the body language."

"I've never really been a student of body language."

68 ≈

"The way she's leaning back."

"Ah."

"And the way she's keeping her arms folded across her chest."

"Ummm."

"Definitely not a romance."

"I wish you were as good at mind reading as you are at interpreting body language."

"Why?"

"Then we'd know what they're doing together. And who they are."

"I guess that would kind of help."

Tobin shrugged and went back to his scotch and soda. The redhead and the older man had started talking quietly and there wasn't much reason to watch them any longer.

"Hey!" shouted the lounge singer in the gold lamé dinner jacket. "It's time for another tribute!"

"Time for another tribute?" Tobin said. "The bastard just finished one two minutes ago."

"Joey Dee and the Starlighters!" cried the singer as he assumed immediately the Twist position.

The name of the tabloid the redhead, Iris Graves, worked for was *Snoop*. Presently it sold a little more than three million copies a week and it enhanced its considerable newsstand revenues with advertising for hemorrhoid products and truss products and products for people who wet their pants and products for people who couldn't see so well and products for people who couldn't hear a damn word if you stood right next to them and screamed and products for people who wanted even a few more mementos of Elvis and products for people who enjoyed American flag coasters and American flag clocks and American flag socks. The biggest issue they'd ever done was estimating the number of "major Hollywood stars" who were rumored to have AIDS. (One office pundit saying, "If we could just tie UFOs into this somehow, we'd have a 99 percent sell-through.")

All of which made it virtually impossible for Iris to convince anybody that she was a bona-fide journalist. The thirty-seven-year-old beauty (and beauty she was and never forgot it) was a reporter for *Snoop*, but she was also holder of an M.A. in journalism from Harvard, former feature writer for the *Chicago Tribune*, and decliner of at least three hundred pitches to go into TV news—despite the fact that the camera would have gone sappy over her Hepburnish cheekbones and chills-down-the-spine smile. She wanted to have *fun* being a journalist and sitting behind an anchor desk was hardly her idea of that. So when *Snoop*'s president, the surprisingly earnest J. H. Hoolihan, a shanty Irish muckraker who now got to put his fat white ass on the surface of a gold inlaid bathtub the size of a garage floor, offered her a job, she'd been, in equal parts, offended and intrigued. Her newspaper friends all ridiculed the idea, of course, and even her father seemed troubled by her impending decision ("Would you really want to see the Graves name on a paper like that, honey?"). But in the end, far more fascinated than she should have been, she took the job. And began learning about a new way of perceiving reality.

While most of what *Snoop* reported was not true in the absolute sense, almost everything it reported was true in *some* sense. If so-and-so was not having an affair with so-and-so, there was a good chance that they had spent some idle time together. If the latest cancer findings were not exactly a breakthrough, then at least they offered some new hope. And if the cop in New Jersey did not see a UFO exactly, he saw *some* goddamn thing. And so it went. Not the truth exactly but not a lie exactly either. And it sure beat covering city council meetings and fashion shows and Pet News. For instance, the story—scandal, really—she was working on now . . .

"You're tense tonight, darlin'."

"I've told you, Sanderson. Don't call me darlin'. I hate that."

"You're really one of them, aren't you?"

"One of whom?"

"Libbers."

"Oh, Christ."

"You deny it?"

"No, I don't deny it." She laughed.

"I don't appreciate being mocked, little girl."

"I just didn't know anybody actually said that anymore."

"Said what?"

"'Libbers.' And especially in that tone. Sort of like 'Communist.'"

She'd made him angry and she knew it and she didn't give the slightest damn. When you were born beautiful and your father had oodles and you maintained a 3.8 all the way through grad school, there was very little you did give the slightest damn about.

He leaned forward, all cheap aftershave and cigarette smoke, and made his face mean. "You seem to forget I could have you arrested for what you did to me."

"You'd have to prove it."

"Oh, I could prove it, darlin'. I could prove it."

She felt sad suddenly. She liked sitting here in the shadows of the stage, most of the people in evening clothes, a band providing lots of festive noise. She just wished she were with a man she enjoyed. Sanderson was too old for her, too stupid, too crude. The only reason she sat with him now was because he'd seen her the other night when, dressed in snap-brim fedora and trench coat, she left the cabin of Cindy McBain, where the dead Ken Norris lay on the floor.

He'd insisted on her coming back to his cabin. She'd been prepared to give into him, of course, and assumed she knew without asking what he wanted—sex. If she didn't give in he'd go to the captain—and would the captain actually believe her story that she'd dressed up this way only so she could follow Ken Norris in pursuit of her story? And then sneaked into the room only after somebody had knocked her out while she hid on deck, watching the cabin? The only reason she'd sneaked in was because she sensed that something was terribly wrong and she'd been right. Then the bathroom door had opened and Cindy had come out and Iris had panicked and pushed past her and gone out into the night and . . .

But Sanderson hadn't wanted sex. He'd said, in fact, "Been married to the same woman for forty-one years. Never slept with another one. Had a chance to once, Louisiana—it was right after the Korean War—but I turned her down. Man gives his word it should stay gived."

Then Sanderson had said, "I don't believe you killed that man but I want to know what you were doing in that cabin."

She'd told him she was a reporter. She'd told him for whom. She'd told him she was working on a story. What she didn't tell him was what the story was all about, or whom it involved.

And that's what he was still trying to find out.

Now Sanderson said, "You got two hours left."

"I'm aware of that."

"Two hours and either you give me the name of the person you're following or I go to the captain."

"Who are you, Sanderson? What's your interest in this?"

"Darlin', you're in no position to be askin' me any questions."

"You can only push it so far, Sanderson."

He smiled. He had been handsome once but now there was too much age and malice in his gaze for that. "And just how far would that be, darlin'?"

"Which one is it?" she asked.

"Which one?"

"It's one of them on 'Celebrity Circle,' isn't it?"

He intentionally made his voice naïve. "Now, darlin', what would I want with one of them celebrities?"

"You've got something on one of them, don't you? That's why you're on this ship."

"Now why would you think that?"

"Because I followed you yesterday afternoon."

For the first time, his face showed real interest in what she was saying. A sense of caution tightened his voice. "Followed me?"

"Yes."

"In the afternoon?"

"Yes."

"And what was I doin', darlin'?"

"You were sliding a number ten white envelope under the door of each celebrity—with the exception of Tobin."

"And why do you suppose I wouldn't include Tobin?"

"Because he isn't one of them. They've been together a long time and he's just a guest."

"You're a very intelligent woman, darlin'. But I imagine you're a mighty frustrated one too."

She expected a sexual remark. He surprised her. "Because you know deep down that I'm not goin' to tell you bird squat about what I'm doin' on this ship." Then he laughed. It was a merry laugh.

"And you're not going to find out what I'm doing on this ship, either."

Then he startled her.

She sat there with her Harvard degree and her beauty and her daddy's wealth thinking what a crude clod Sanderson was, and then he startled her completely.

He told her exactly what she was doing on this ship. Exactly.

And then he started laughing again.

Merrily.

"You bastard," she said. "How did you find out?"

"I've got a lot of surprises in me, darlin'," he said, hoisting his wineglass. "A lot of them."

Around 9:00 the entertainment got much better. Marty Gerber, the comic, took the large semicircular stage with a baby blue spot and a painting of Eden in the background. He had rarely been this good, his timing flawless, and his material confessional without being self-indulgent (the difference between Robert Klein and Richard Lewis), and the diners responded accordingly.

By now, Tobin and Cindy were bombed, though Cindy kept denying it. "God, Tobin, can't I even have a few drinks and relax?"

"I wasn't criticizing. I merely mentioned that when you got up to go to the bathroom the last time, you sort of wobbled."

"Wobbled? I wobbled? I don't wobble, Tobin. I really don't. I don't weigh enough to wobble, for one thing."

"Now I know you're drunk."

"How?"

"Because wobbling doesn't have anything to do with weight."

"Then what does it have to do with?"

"I'm not sure but it's definitely not weight."

"You're the one who's drunk."

"I am, true enough. But at least I admit it."

"Well, when I get drunk, Tobin, I'll admit it too." At which point she knocked over her drink. "Don't say anything, Tobin."

He didn't, and instead turned his attention back to Marty Gerber. As he watched, he got into one of his generous moods—certain nights riding high he felt positively Old Testament patriarchal, sort of like Pa in a biblical version of "Bonanza"—and started concocting all sorts of plans about how he'd write this column about this great young comedian and how, within twenty-four hours of the column appearing, Marty would be signing for his own HBO special.

Then his good mood waned because he happened to see, far back in the shadows of the restaurant, the makeup girl, Joanna Howard. She sat alone at a tiny table and stared as much at the wall as at the stage. She ate her food quickly, as if she couldn't wait to jump up and leave. She wore a pretty, very formal long-sleeved white blouse and what appeared to be a rather gaudy pink skirt. Her hair was pulled into a severe bun and she wore glasses.

He said, "You mind if I go say hi to somebody?"

"Who?"

"God."

"What?"

"That was just supposed to be a rhetorical question."

"Huh?" She really was plastered. Kansas City was bombed out of her mind.

"I was supposed to say, 'Do you mind if I go see somebody?' and you were supposed to say 'No, of course not.'"

"I don't want you to leave me alone."

"You'll be fine."

"They'll all start looking at me again."

"It's because you're so beautiful."

"I'm not beautiful. I'm volup—" She couldn't say it. "You know what I mean."

"Well, you are voluptuous, but you've also got a great face."

"That isn't why they'll look at me. They'll look at me because the captain keeps telling everybody that I killed Ken Norris."

"You'll be fine. I'll only be gone for a minute."

"I'll count to sixty and you'd better be back."

He rose, kissed her on the forehead, and then made his way through the tables.

A few people gave him the "celebrity stare," one invariably tainted with disappointment. When you first meet someone who's on TV, that person assumes a stature he can't possibly have in reality. Tobin was this five-five guy with red hair—TV hid that fact, or at least made it more interesting than it was.

When he reached her table and she looked up, she seemed almost frightened. He thought of Cindy and her body language theories. It did not take a Ph.D. in the subject to realize that the way Joanna Howard tried to shrink down meant that she did not want visitors.

"Hi."

"Hi," she said.

"I just wondered if you'd like to join us." He waved in the general vicinity of Cindy.

"Oh, no. That's all right."

He was drunk enough to say it straight out. "You look so lonely."

"I am lonely." She smiled. "But I don't think sitting at your table is going to help me." She paused. "I'm not trying to be rude."

"Everybody's having so much fun."

She shook her head. "Everybody's having so much fun—and Ken Norris is dead less than twenty-four hours." She stared at him in her unscrubbed, earnest way and he felt moved by her gaze at that moment, almost jarred by it. "We don't give a damn about each other. We really don't."

Behind him now the laughter sounded hedonistic and pagan. He wanted to share her grief—whatever its source—for he recognized it as the same sort of grief he carried around. The difference was he had his writing and his drinking and his remorse to keep the grief at bay. She didn't seem to have much at all except the two cheap rings on her skinny fingers and the frilly blouse on her frail torso and the girly confusion in her eyes. He wanted to cradle her and violate her at the same time. My God, he was drunk.

"Your friend," she said.

"My friend?" He was confused.

"Your dinner date." She pointed.

"Oh. Yes."

"She looks angry."

"Oh?"

"She's been glaring over here."

"She's very drunk."

"And you're not?"

"Do I seem drunk?"

"You're weaving."

"Ah."

"Did I insult you?"

"No. I just got finished telling her she was wobbling. Now you're telling me I'm weaving."

"She really does look angry. Maybe you'd better get back to her."

"You're the smartest makeup person I've ever known." He wanted it to be a compliment. Instead he'd only sounded silly. But then he often sounded silly, didn't he?

"See you in the morning on the set," Joanna said.

"You're invited to join us. Just walk over any time."

"Thank you."

Then he turned—damn, he really was weaving—and started back through the obstacle course of tables. The least thing they could do—management, that is—was put the things in a straight line so a guy wouldn't have to bruise his hips by bumping into chair after chair and table after table.

"You were gone over four minutes," Cindy said when he got back.

"How would you know? You don't have a watch."

"I counted the seconds."

"So did I and I was barely gone three minutes."

"You said one."

"If the tables had been in a straight line, I would've been back much sooner."

"Huh?"

"You say that a lot, you know that?"

"Say what a lot?"

"'Huh.' You say 'Huh' an awful lot."

And then the slap came and it was loud as a car backfiring, so loud it broke Marty Gerber's rhythm completely, and he fell silent at once.

The "Celebrity Circle" panel and their mates had all been dining at one long table to the right of the stage. Given their "star" status, the table was decorated with colorful flowers as well as long, tapering candles that seemed to imbue the darkness with a special glow. Invariably, their meal was interrupted by tourists stopping by like hungry animals to chat or joke or have their picture snapped with their favorite personality. When you haven't been on network television for a while, you're generally glad you get such treatment, even though you might pretend otherwise.

But something had gone wrong.

Cassie McDowell had slapped Todd Ames with a terrific left hand and now was on her feet. "At least don't be a hypocrite, Todd! You got his job! You can't be too unhappy he's dead—and anyway, every one of us wanted him dead. Every one of us!"

Then she fell to sobbing. The dark-haired Susan Richards stood up and took the younger woman into her arms, letting her spill a considerable amount of tears on her naked shoulder—Susan wore a strapless white gown that even the unfashionable Tobin could see was a tad out of date.

"God," Cindy McBain said. "She's really crazy. Cassie, I mean. Why would they all want him dead?"

"I don't know. But in the morning I think I'll find out."

From the stage, Marty Gerber was saying, "Hey, isn't that just like actors? Give us a show even when we don't want it!"

The diners broke into applause for his clever ad-lib.

Todd Ames kept his gray and handsome head down.

Jere Farris and his wife, Alicia, looked humiliated. And the blond strongman Kevin Anderson gave everybody watching them a look at his capped teeth in a public relations textbook smile that tried to pretend everything was fine.

But Tobin's attention turned quickly to the redhead and the man in the western suit.

They'd quit talking and now simply watched the celebrity table. Obviously they were fascinated.

Once again Tobin had the impression that they knew something special—something Tobin should know—but he had no idea what it was.

Only that it undoubtedly involved the notebook Alicia Farris and the redheaded woman had been wrestling over outside his cabin door this afternoon.

"Oh, no," Cindy said.

"What?" Tobin said.

"It's going to happen."

"What's going to happen?"

"When I have four drinks I get slightly drunk and have a very good time. And when I have six drinks my inhibitions sort of go and I—well, you know. I just sort of can't help myself. But when I have seven drinks . . ." Then she paused and shook her head.

"Yes?" Tobin said. "Seven drinks and you do what?"

"I," Cindy said, getting to her feet unsteadily, "barf."

16

They made love of sorts (what would have been called third base back in high school, "I'm sorry, I just can't—you know, so soon after Ken and all, you know, don't you? Aren't you sensitive, Tobin, aren't you?"), this being after Cindy threw up three times and then began lamenting the death of her dog when she'd been eight and how her father had always traveled too much and really never *talked* to her about stuff that mattered and how she'd slept too readily with far too many men and how she really should read more and see a better grade of movies ("I really think Barbra Streisand's a great actress, I can't help it") and how she was two months behind on her Trans-Am car payments because she'd loaned this Kansas City Chief she occasionally dated $1,000 from her savings account so he could help out his brother who was in a jam, and then she told him about the one and only time she'd ever really been in love and how the guy just wouldn't make a commitment and how crazy that was with all the guys chasing after her virtually begging her to marry them and then the one guy she really wanted just really abused her ("But isn't that always the way, Tobin, isn't that always the way?") and some of it interested him and some of it he kind of dozed through and some he felt very sorry for her about and some of it made him feel truly superior to her and that of course made him feel like a complete shit and some of it made no sense at all ("I just keep thinking I'm from this other planet, Tobin; you know, like these aliens dropped me off here and forgot to come back and get me. Do you ever feel like that?"). And anyway what he was truly interested in was her neck (she had a wonderful, graceful, *chewy* kind of neck) and her delightful breasts and her lickable legs and finally, finally he started kissing her and she more or less responded and then they got seminaked on his bed and he liked the way the moonlight came through the louvered windows and the way the salt air smelled and the distant festive music and then kissing her breasts at last and then putting his hand against her warmest part and her saying, between kisses, "I just keep thinking about Ken and all and how promiscuous I've become. I wasn't always this way, I really wasn't, otherwise I'd do it, really, Tobin, I would," and then with that gentlest but most final of female gestures, pushing him away so he could not get inside and saying, "But I really like you, Tobin; you've been so great to me, and you're a celebrity and you don't have to be great to people or anything if you don't want to be." And then about two seconds later he was up like a teenager caught by a girl's enraged mom, up and jerking on his pants and stumbling to the door because somebody was pounding on it and finding there Kevin Anderson, blond and apparently still under the impression that he was a TV cop, saying, "You'd better come up to the deck, Tobin. Something really incredible has happened" and all the while peeking over Tobin's shoulder at the naked form of Cindy writhing about in the shadows back there trying to get dressed. "Something really incredible."

17 Thursday: 12:17 A.M.

There were two of them in deck chairs side by side, the redhead and the man in the western suit. They might have been enjoying a view of the moonlit ocean swelling on the endless line of horizon. Or the clarity of the Big Dipper laced across the ebony tropical sky.

Each of them had been shot several times in the chest. They were very bloody.

They appeared, as dead people usually appeared to Tobin, to be playing a trick of some kind. Any moment now they'd be leaping to their feet and saying they'd only been trying to frighten people.

He edged Cindy a little closer to the bodies. They did not seem to have been bound in any way. They just sat in their chairs with their eyes fixed in the general vicinity of the Big Dipper.

A semicircle of passengers stared at the corpses with a mixture of awe, terror, and bewilderment. There were tears, of course—soft and childlike, without anger because apparently no one here had known these two people—and there were furious glances at Captain Hackett, who stood among a group of white-uniformed stewards whom he was dispatching to various tasks with an air of sweaty purpose that might soon become—unthinkable for the placid captain—real panic.

The chairs in which the dead people sat were adjacent to one of the ship's three pools. The water was aqua. The tartness of chlorine was in the air. When Tobin looked back at the assembled passengers—some were in pajamas and robes and nightgowns and some still wore neckties or loud Hawaiian shirts from any number of private or public parties—he felt his first bit of sympathy ever for Capt. Robert Hackett. The ship was three days out with four more days to go before port. And now there could be no doubt about it. There was a killer on board and this time it would do no good whatsoever to point a finger at a beautiful secretary from Kansas City, Missouri.

"There's that doctor," Cindy McBain whispered to Tobin.

A stolid, brown-haired man in a white shirt and dark slacks and white deck shoes came up the steps from the deck below and walked over to the bodies. He nodded to several of the stewards and then started talking to the captain.

Tobin glanced around at the crowd and, not seeing who he was looking for, said, "Cindy, would you mind waiting here?"

"For what?"

"I forgot something in the room."

"Forgot what?"

"Gee, I'm glad you don't ask a lot of questions."

"Well, you're lying to me, Tobin."

He sighed. "I need to go find somebody."

"Who?"

"Alicia Farris."

"The producer's wife?"

"Right."

"Why?"

"I'm not sure."

"Bull."

"I'm not. I mean, I just want to ask her what she knew about the red-haired woman."

"And you can't take me with you?"

"It'll be easier if I go alone."

"Thanks a lot."

"I'm sorry but it will."

Now she sighed. "All right."

"C'mon, Cindy. I'm really not trying to hurt your feelings."

"I know."

"I won't be long. I promise."

She made a little flouncing motion, as if her entire body had simply given in to his deserting her. "Just go on, Tobin. Just go on."

Not even after Ken Norris's murder had Tobin thought of all the neat places a killer could hide aboard a cruise ship but now as he made his way down two decks and along shadowy passageways, he realized that, especially late at night, a killer would have no problem at all hiding and then fleeing back to his or her room. No problem at all.

When he came to the Farrises' cabin, he put his ear to the door before knocking.

Inside he heard drawers being opened and closed hurriedly. It did not seem likely either Jere or Alicia Farris would frantically search through their own drawers—not unless they were planning to go someplace . . . and where could they go in the middle of the ocean?

He moved away from the door and pressed himself against the wall.

More drawers were jerked open, slammed shut. Closet doors on rollers were hurled back. Then, more faintly, things in the bathroom medicine cabinet were pushed around.

All Tobin could do was wait.

Two minutes later the door squeaked open and a figure he did not at first recognize moved out into the hallway.

True to TV movie fashion, the figure wore a dark beret, a dark sweater, a dark jacket, dark socks, and dark shoes.

Unfortunately, her hair was not dark but dishwater blond.

He got her by the wrist. "You're the last person I would have suspected of being a thief."

Joanna Howard, the quiet makeup girl, glanced up at him and said, "Oh, God, Mr. Tobin, are you going to tell anybody?"

From the opposite end of the hall, he could hear passengers coming. This corridor was no place to talk.

He kept hold of her wrist. "Come on," he said.

"I don't know why she started suspecting us," Joanna Howard said ten minutes later.

Tobin had gone to one of the lounges and gotten them diet 7-Ups. He puffed on a cigarillo and let her explain.

"This is Alicia, you mean."

"Yes."

"Suspecting what?"

"The fact that Jere and I were having an affair."

"You and Jere?"

She smiled, looking sad as she did so. "I know, neither one of us are likely types, are we?"

Tobin shrugged. They stood on the sports deck watching the ocean churn behind them. He was chilly.

"Unfortunately for the institution of marriage," Tobin said, "everybody seems to be the type at one point or another."

"It wasn't sleazy."

"I'm not saying it was."

"And it wasn't just a one-night sort of thing."

"I don't imagine it was."

"And I really think we may love each other. We've talked about it, anyway." She paused and glared at him. "What's so funny?"

"The idea of talking over if you're in love or not. I'm not sure that's necessary. It seems to me you're either in love or you're not."

"That's because you've had so many affairs, Mr. Tobin. Jere and I—well, we're not really experienced." She flushed. "He's my first real lover and even though he won't exactly admit it, I think Alicia was the first woman he ever slept with." In her beret and dark clothes, she was fetching. But how sad she looked leaning against the railing with the furious white wake waters below them, the dark and silver ocean covering all else.

"You could get hurt."

"He wouldn't do that to me, Mr. Tobin."

"He might not want to but he might have to."

"If he decides to stay with her, you mean?"

"Yes."

"I'm prepared for that." But there was a catch in her throat and Tobin knew better.

"So why were you in their room?"

"Because I'd acted impulsively. Stupidly, really."

"Tell me."

"I'd . . . I'd been afraid of exactly what you were talking about."

"Of being dumped?"

"Yes."

"And?"

"And so tonight I wrote him a letter. It was a very . . . it was kind of a real blunt letter."

"Telling him you love him?"

"Yes."

"And telling him you want a decision right away?"

"Yes."

He smiled and slid his arm around her shoulder. "Joanna, we've all written letters like that. We get lonely and scared and it's only natural."

"Yes, but I made the mistake of sliding it under his door because he told me Alicia was going to a party tonight and that he was just going to go to bed. They don't have a very good relationship and do a lot of things alone like that." She paused, shook her head. "So I pushed it under the door and knocked, hoping he'd wake up and see it. Then I went back to my cabin and waited for a phone call. I thought he'd read it and call me right away. I mean, I figured my knock had awakened him for sure. But then no call came. I waited for nearly two hours. Then I got this terrible feeling. What if he changed his mind at the last minute and went to the party and when they got back to their room they would find my letter on the floor? She'd see it for sure."

"So you sneaked back to their room. How'd you get in?"

"Credit card."

"Really?"

"One of the crew showed me how to do it."

"Nice crew."

"But it wasn't there."

"The letter?"

"No."

"And that's why you were tossing the room?"

"You mean opening drawers and stuff?"

"Right."

"I just went crazy. Started throwing stuff around and . . . I really got scared. If she ever saw a letter like that she'd—she'd have proof then, not just suspicions."

"So you didn't find the letter?"

"No."

He said, "Two more people were murdered tonight."

He wasn't sure why, but he was very interested in her reaction. "Who?"

He told her. "Did you know or speak with either of them ever?"

"No." Then she seemed to understand his motive. "You think I had something to do with it, Mr. Tobin?"

He laughed and touched her shoulder again. "No, I don't, Joanna." He glanced at his watch. He'd left Cindy alone now for nearly half an hour. He said, "Did you put the room back in order?"

"Yes. I was very careful."

"Then all you can do is wait."

"What if she came back for something and found it on the floor?"

He leaned over and kissed her on the forehead. "There are all sorts of possibilities and every one of them will make you crazy if you think of it too long. So why not go have a drink somewhere and wait till you hear from Jere? That's really about all you can do now."

This time she touched him. "You're really nice, Mr. Tobin. I'd heard a lot of stories about you, but." She stopped herself. "Well, you know, everybody tells stories about everybody."

"I know," Tobin said. "'Yosemite Sam.'"

She giggled. "Coming from you, it sounds funny."

Suddenly all Tobin wanted was to go back and find

Cindy. To hell with murders. To hell with this young woman's love affair.

"I'll walk you back to your cabin," Tobin said.

"See," she said, "you really are nice."

He took her to her cabin and said good-night and said to try and get some sleep and then he went back to the deck where the bodies had been found.

The passengers were gone, and so were the corpses, and so were the captain and the stewards in white uniforms.

And so was Cindy.

He checked his own cabin and then he checked her cabin and then he tried a few of the lounges where, of course, the murders were the number one topic. In one of the lounges he saw a crew member and described Cindy to him and asked if he'd seen her and the guy said, "Oh, the babe from Kansas City? God, isn't she all right?" He shrugged. "She was in here a while ago but she left."

"Alone?"

"Huh-uh. With everybody's least favorite TV cop."

"You're kidding? Kevin Anderson?"

"Right." He grinned. "Why would she take him when she could have had me without hardly begging at all?"

18 3:14 A.M.

He didn't find her. He checked out her cabin several times and he checked out the various lounges but he didn't find her and he recalled once a high school girlfriend who'd made him unbelievably jealous, and how in his battered Ford he used to drive around and around her house, knowing she was out on a date with someone else, there being a kind of solace in the mere motion of driving around and around her house, there having been no solace in anything else during those terrible nights, knowing she was irretrievably gone from him. He hated being jealous, the way it demeaned him, but he never seemed able to escape its clutches long. He had been known to get jealous during the first ten minutes of a blind date when, at a party, his date had seen an old boyfriend and merely nodded, proving to Tobin (as he had admitted to Dr. Spengler during six useless months on the couch) that he was probably at least 37.8 percent crazy after all.

He went back to his cabin and stripped and lay down and took his emergency cigarette from his dinner jacket and, of course, being months old, it was hard and stale but Tobin tried not to notice that as he sat on the edge of his bed in his underwear inhaling the thing, thinking of Cindy in the arms of Kevin Anderson and wishing that he were not five-five and not so complicated and that Cindy and he could fall madly in love for the remaining three days of the cruise. It was testament to his frame of mind that he only rarely thought about the bodies he'd seen earlier on the deck, or about the dead Ken Norris.

And then, cigarette half-smoked and already starting to feel guilty about his indulgence ("Now isn't that a stupid reaction to something like Cindy dumping you—smoking? Exactly who did it help? You? Anybody? No."), a knock like a rock fell on the door and of course he thought: Cindy. She's spent enough time with the TV playboy and is sorry and now at last we're going to make love and spend three fleshy, blissful days together.

But it wasn't Cindy at the door. Not at all.

It was Captain Hackett.

19

4:34 A.M.

"Small caliber bullets, close range."

"Dr. Devane used to be a coroner," Captain Hackett explained. "He's now a full-time physician aboard the ship."

"I see," Tobin said.

"Upstate New York," the doctor said. "Where I was a coroner, I mean." He seemed to think his former address had some bearing here. He was the same brown-haired man Tobin had seen on deck earlier. He wore a blue suit and a white button-down shirt and a red tie. He looked like a politician. He had the teeth for it, anyway, and that odd, cold distance Tobin had always sensed in politicians.

They were in Captain Hackett's office, sitting at a round table covered with rolled-up nautical maps. A decanter of brandy and three glasses were on the table. A facsimile of a Chesterfield lamp was pulled down near their heads for illumination. In the portholes the night was velvet black. None of the men could be said to be quite sober.

"Do you know who they were?" Tobin said.

"The woman's name was Iris Graves." The captain poured each of them more brandy as he spoke.

"Know anything about her?"

"I've been through her belongings. She seemed to be a reporter."

"Really?"

"Yes. And you won't believe for what paper." The captain laughed. *"Snoop."*

"That thing in the supermarket?" the doctor said.

"Exactly."

"The hell of it is," Tobin said, "they sometimes get things right. Or half right." Then he thought back to her wrestling match with Alicia Farris. The notebook they'd been fighting over became very large in Tobin's mind. "How about the man?"

"Sanderson. Everett Sanderson."

"Occupation?"

"Not sure."

"You went through his things?"

"Yes. But except for a few letters addressed to him, there was no other form of identification," the captain said. "Plus he bought his ticket under the name of Kelly."

"Why would he do that?" the doctor said. He sounded irritated at the mere thought of dishonest people.

"That's what we're going to find out," the captain said. "Or presumably, anyway."

Tobin said, "I'm waiting for the good part, Captain."

"'The good part?'"

"Yes, when you tell me why you invited me to your cabin."

Captain Hackett leaned forward beneath the Chesterfield light and folded his hands. Tobin recalled the man's panic earlier in the evening—the first indication that he was perhaps not as composed as he hoped to appear. "I need a spy, Mr. Tobin."

"A spy."

"We've got three and a half days before we reach port. That means for three days I need to keep several hundred passengers calm. I need to find out what's going on."

"I don't understand what I can do."

"You're in a unique position. You're one of them but you're not one of them."

"One of whom?"

"The 'Celebrity Circle' crowd. You're part of the show but you're not intimate with any of them. I've noticed that you don't take your meals with them and that you don't go to their parties and that you don't hang out with them much."

Tobin shrugged. "I'm a guest 'celebrity.' They're a very tight-knit little group."

Without reservation, the captain said, "One of them is a killer."

"That's a pretty heavy accusation."

"I have no doubt it's true. Especially since I found out that the Graves woman was a reporter." He paused again and glanced at the doctor. "Naturally, we've got security forces of our own aboard the vessel, Mr. Tobin, but as I said, you're in a unique position to find some things out."

"Right now I'm very interested in Sanderson."

"So am I. I've already put in a call to our home office. We should know a great deal more about him within eight hours or so."

"The biggest problem you're going to have, Robert," the doctor said, "is keeping everybody calm." He made a face at Tobin and Tobin realized just how drunk the man was. "Including me." The doctor laughed, but he was only half-joking. "I sure as hell don't like walking around a cruise ship where a killer's loose. Do you, Mr. Tobin?"

"So how about it?" the captain said.

"I'll help you any way I can," Tobin said. "I mean, if I find anything out, I'll let you know."

"I'd appreciate it if you'd go out of your way to find things out."

"All right."

"And report them back to me."

"Of course."

"Because one more murder and . . ." The captain shook his head. "The cruise industry can be very profitable, Mr. Tobin. It can also become very unprofitable once you start getting a certain reputation."

The drunken doctor said, "I think you can understand our position."

What he actually said was, "I shink y'can unnershand our poshishion."

Tobin was just glad the good doctor wasn't performing surgery this evening.

Or that Tobin wasn't going to be his patient, anyway.

Tobin went through the special hell of insomnia. Why is it, he wondered, when you can't sleep you don't have sexual fantasies about gorgeous women but instead concentrate on all the terrible things you've done with your life? Your failures. Your excesses. Your petty vanities.

Sick of flowered shirts, he put on a plain white button-down job, a pair of Lee jeans, and his blue canvas slip-on deck shoes, and went out to the railing to watch the rolling water and the way the moonlight burnished its black and eternal beauty.

Now the human sounds were gone and there was just the steady thrum of the powerful engines and the caw of occasional birds lost in the midnight clouds.

"Seems that we have the same problem."

He was embarrassed by the way he started at the unexpected sound of another voice.

She lay a soft hand on his elbow and said, "Gosh, I didn't mean to frighten you."

He relaxed, smiled. "Just lost in my thoughts, I guess."

"Pleasant thoughts, I hope," Susan Richards said. She wore a white robe that gave her already delicate beauty an almost spectral cast. He thought, being a movie critic, of the painting of Laura in Preminger's great film, and then he realized, in his heart rather than his groin, that ever since meeting her a few days ago he'd had a somewhat active crush on Susan.

She joined him, leaning on her elbows at the railing. She smelled wonderfully of skin lotion and perfume.

He laughed. "I wish they *were* pleasant, Susan. I'm afraid at this time of night, all I can think of is what a jerk I've been with people I've loved."

She was in profile, perfect profile, but still he could see how his words affected her. A slight jolt of the body, as if she'd been struck. The shadow of melancholy falling across the eye and mouth. "We all have those regrets, Tobin." She turned to him gently. Were there soft tears in her eyes? "And you never get rid of them, no matter how many people you surround yourself with, or how much noise you create."

"I see you know what I'm talking about."

"Of course."

They turned their attention back to the silvery water, to the endless night. At such moments the mere notion of daylight seemed impossible. It would always be night, and a world of whispers and shadows, and guilt.

He felt, wanting her, feckless as an eighth-grader.

He let his elbow touch her elbow just the tiniest bit and she startled him completely by taking his hand.

"Do you like holding hands?"

"I love holding hands," he said.

"Good, then let's hold hands and watch the water and not talk, all right?"

His heart, his groin, and perhaps his entire soul seemed to be logjammed in his throat. He gulped and said with a cracking eighth-grade voice, "Fine."

While he didn't talk, he did watch her, the beauty that was so easy to see yet so remote in some way he could not understand but only sense. Her hand was silken and beneath the tender flesh he felt the delicate bones and small tendons of her fingers. God, he was so dizzy, it really was like eighth grade, words and the proper moves lost to him.

She spoke first. "Wouldn't it be nice to take a lifeboat and row to an island somewhere, one of those islands Gauguin liked to paint, and just live there peacefully the rest of your life?" Tears were still evident in her voice, and a subtle hint of desperation.

He was thinking of her, of going to that island with her, and for a moment his self-loathing was gone and he saw them in some ridiculous but fetching movie as island mates, tummies pleasantly filled with the fish he'd speared earlier that afternoon in waters blue as Aqua Velva, and making love on a bed of gigantic green palm fronds near a crystal waterfall.

"I'd leave in a minute," he said. Then he brought her to him and started to kiss her, trying to make his move gentle and tender, rather than threatening or overtly sexual.

But she crossed her slender arms in front of her so he could not get close enough to kiss her. "I don't mean to be a tease," she said.

"It's all right. I shouldn't have done that."

"Well, for what it's worth, a part of me wanted you to do that."

He let her go. "I think I'd rather wait till *all* of you wants me to do that."

She took his hand again and held it to her face and for some reason, he thought of a small beautiful child hugging her brown fuzzy teddy bear.

Her eyes were closed in unfathomable yearning and she said, her voice slight and nearly lost in the sudden caw of ocean birds again, "I think I can sleep now. I think I can now."

She left.

It was both abrupt and graceful, her departure, and he was struck again with the word *spectral*, because she was so much the lovely ghost as her white robe faded, faded down the gloom of the deck until she was one completely with the darkness, not even the slap of her slippers or the scent of her perfume left as tangible evidence of her existence.

He stayed there, as if just banished from Eden, not knowing what to do with himself or the quick doom of his feelings for Susan Richards.

Finally he went back to his cabin and fell into uneasy sleep.

20 10:43 A.M.

In the morning three episodes of "Celebrity Circle" were shot and of the three only the middle one had any sort of spontaneity. Even when the Applause sign ignited there was only a faint slapping together of hands—too many people thinking about the curious couple found dead on the fourth deck. During the second episode, however, a certain bitchy brilliance overtook Cassie McDowell (so much for her "McKinley High, USA" image) and she proceeded to cut sharp and close at the bone of fame, ragging the somewhat pompous Todd Ames about his new hosting job and even skewing some of the "civilian" guests. ("God, is that your real laugh or do you get an extra piece of luggage for cackling that way?") Jere Farris was up on a small tier with the crew. He paced and wrung his hands and then flung helpless looks down at Joanna Howard, who flung them right back up like faded roses at a departing lover. Tobin got to see all this because the civilians who stood to win everything from washers to cars rarely called on him, Tobin being a terrible player. He always panicked and blanked and as Todd was wishing them adieu they always glowered at him, vague threats in their gaze, as if they held him accountable for the fact that their children would never again have enough to eat.

So the morning bloody went.

"I don't suppose you'd tell me what was in that notebook you and Iris Graves were wrestling over yesterday, would you?"

"Oh, God, you really are playing detective, aren't you?"

As he seated himself at Alicia Farris's table in one of the smaller lounges, Tobin had of course expected not only resistance but resentment from Alicia. He hadn't expected her wry, even amused glance.

"Nice place, isn't it?" She smiled. "Makes you want to go get a pan and look for some gold."

The motif here was the gold rush, and all the expected clichés of interior decoration had been brought to bear—blowups of forlorn gold mining camps, waitresses got up to resemble saloon hostesses, wagon wheels mounted on the wall, and drinks served in tin pans with FOOL'S GOLD written on the side. Fortunately, it was pretty dark, so nobody could see Tobin blush. Stuff like this really embarrassed him.

"It's wonderful," he said.

"Now do you want me to tell you what you're wondering?"

"What am I wondering?"

"You're wondering why an otherwise respectable woman such as myself would be sitting alone in a kitschy little lounge having a drink at three in the afternoon."

"Actually, I wasn't wondering that at all."

"Well, in case you hadn't heard, my husband is having an affair."

"I'm sorry." He said it as if she'd just told him her biopsy had been horrible. In a way, he thought, it was sort of the same thing. He had to pretend innocence, of course. If he seemed knowing, she would feel paranoid—as if he were somehow part of a vast conspiracy from which she'd been kept. You got that way when your mate's infidelities became public.

"Oh, he's done it before, Tobin. It's nothing new."

"Still, it can't be much fun."

"You sound as if you know what I'm going through."

"I've been on both ends of that particular gun."

"Well put," she said. Then, "I wish I had. Been on both sides, I mean. To get back at him, I once tried to sleep with a parking lot attendant. He was very beautiful, very brown—he might have been part Negro—and we got so far as his shabby little apartment and I felt ashamed and excited at the same time and then his girlfriend came in. She was *very* brown—and very angry. She slapped him and then she slapped me and I realized what a silly suburban white woman I was after all and I just ran and ran. One of my heels came off but I kept running down the street anyway, limping, and finally a cop stopped me and asked if I was all right and I said no I wasn't all right, and then I began crying and it was really terrible, right there in the sunlight—it was very hot and very bright—just sobbing and all these fascinated street people gathering around to watch me come undone, and this cop just held me as if he were my father, and just let me cry and it was so decent of him that I just cried all the more and . . ."

She took a bitter drag of her cigarette. This afternoon she wore a tan blouse and white slacks. She also wore large wooden hoop earrings. Her makeup was flawless. She was still overweight but oddly her weight gave her a real poise and dignity. "He always goes to the same sort."

"Jere?"

"Ummmm."

"What sort is that?"

"You're not having a drink?" she asked, as a waiter dressed up as an old sourdough approached. Tobin, seeing his costume, wanted, most uncivilly, to punch him out. "Diet 7-Up," Tobin said, not looking at the poor kid, who was probably working his way through college. He noticed the way fortyish and overweight Alicia touched the very tip of her tongue to the center of her red upper lip. There was a certain Victorian eroticism about it and he fell for a painful moment to remembering that Cindy McBain had spent the night with Kevin Anderson. "What sort?" he said finally.

"Helpless. The opposite of me. I'm his surrogate mother." The rancor of the deserted mate coarsened her voice. "And I was from the beginning."

"How did you meet?"

She smiled and he saw a flash of the girl in her and rather liked the sight of that girl. "I was a continuity person. Or script girl, as they were called in those days. This was down in Falsworth, Georgia, don't you know." She gave him the benefit of a parody southern accent. Tobin wondered why white northern straight people could never quote blacks, southerners, or homosexuals without resorting to dialects and stereotypes. "It was a low-budget movie and Jere was the director. This was when he was right out of film school at USC, his dues-paying period. He'd tried to get some kind of work with Roger Corman—that's when Brian DePalma and Jack Nicholson and Martin Scorsese were working with Corman—but it just never worked out. So he got offered this kind of second unit job with this very low-budget horror movie being shot in Georgia and he took it. On the way down there, the director died of a heart attack so the production company—the people who had hired me—promoted Jere to director. That's where we all met, as a matter of fact—Todd Ames, Ken Norris, Kevin Anderson."

"You've known each other that long? Since. . . ?"

"Since 1968." She laughed. It was a warm feminine laugh and he wanted to kiss her on the forehead. "God, you should have heard us then, Tobin. We were so pretentious. The movie we made . . ." The laugh again. Now he heard the melancholy in it. "Really terrible. 'Ingmar Bergman meets The Monsters,' *Variety* said. And they were being kind."

"And you've been with Jere ever since?"

"Oh, yes. I took out adoption papers shortly after." She stubbed out one cigarette and immediately lit another. "Am I sounding bitchy?"

"Within tolerable limits."

"He's a child."

"Why don't you leave him?"

"I love him. Isn't that the shits?"

"It happens."

"I'm so sensible. Look at these hands." She put her large hands across the table, next to the little electric "kerosene" lamp (probably just the sort real gold miners had used) for his inspection. "Big hands, aren't they?"

"But nicely shaped."

"'Purposeful hands.' That's a line from Steinbeck. I've always liked that. It seemed to describe me exactly." She exhaled. The smoke was a beautiful electric blue in the shadowy bar. They seemed out of time and place here—as if they'd been trapped in some time warp. He did not mind the feeling at all. He thought about ordering a drink but chose not to, knowing he'd only be potzed by dinner.

"Anyway," she said, "I've had to be purposeful for both of us. When he couldn't get work in pictures, I convinced him to go into television. That's how we wound up with 'Celebrity Circle.' We saw Ken and Kevin and Todd all lose their series and so then we heard about this game show packager and we went to them and—well, 'Celebrity Circle' was born. It's been our bread and butter for eight years. And as you can see, it's fed some of us pretty well."

She seemed to want a compliment and he was happy to give her one. "You're a good-looking woman and you know it."

"Do you want to have an affair?"

He laughed. "If we do have an affair, will you tell me why you were wrestling with Iris Graves outside my room the other day?"

"Oh, that, Tobin." She tried to sound dismissive but she couldn't. Not quite. "She's been a pest the past few months. Just trying to dig up some gossip on our show for that rag she works for."

"What was the notebook?"

"I don't know."

"You don't know?"

"I really don't. I'd just had an argument with Jere in our cabin about dear little Joanna Howard and I was walking down the corridor toward the swimming pool and I saw her in a deck chair taking notes and . . . Well, I'd had a few drinks, to be honest, and I just got irrational. I wanted to take her notebook and rip it up. Suddenly the notebook became very symbolic of everything she did and everything that filthy newspaper stands for. Believe me, Tobin, I don't wish *Snoop* on my worst enemy. So anyway, I grabbed the notebook from her and started running down the corridor and she came after it. She grabbed me and we started fighting and that's when you came out." She blew out some more blue smoke. There was just the darkness and the frail light of the fake kerosene lamps and the smell of afternoon indulgence and liquor. "Hardly what my mother would call ladylike behavior." Then she paused. "But if you're asking me am I sorry she was murdered, of course I am." She looked at him boldly. Her wooden earrings clattered. "And I didn't have anything to do with it. Nothing."

"Have you thought any more about Ken Norris and why anybody would want to kill him?"

"I've thought about it but I don't know why."

Someday there would be a machine more reliable than a polygraph and you could just hook people up to it and it would tell you if the person was lying to you or not. Until then you had to depend on your own instincts and they could be pretty damned unreliable. He stared at her and again felt a little fillip of middle-aged desire and then wondered if she were lying and had no idea at all.

"Do you think they're connected—Ken's death and the other two?" she asked.

"Probably," Tobin said.

"Did they find out who the man was?"

"Somebody named Sanderson." Which reminded him that he wanted to go to the captain's office and find out what Hackett had learned about Sanderson. He eased his chair back.

"You're leaving?"

"Afraid I have to," Tobin said.

"Dance with me tonight?"

"Tonight?"

"The costume party."

"Oh. That's right."

"You don't have a costume?"

"I'll probably just wear a raincoat and go as a flasher."

"Will you flash me?"

"I don't think you need an affair right now, Alicia," he said. "I think you need to decide if Jere's worth all the trouble or not."

"He's actually quite a good lover."

"I'm happy to hear that."

"And a very attentive mate when he wants to be."

"Another good quality."

"But he needs a mother and I'm tired of playing the role." She watched Tobin as he stood up and then she said, "I'm not very brave, am I, Tobin?"

"That's the hell of it."

"What?"

"None of us are."

21

Several times—and at perhaps too great a length—Tobin had made the argument in print and on television alike that Rudolph Mate's *D.O.A,* with Edmond O'Brien, and Robert Aldrich's *Kiss Me, Deadly* were two of the greatest film noirs ever made. He believed this so much that he took them with him whenever he traveled, and dipped into them for fifteen or twenty minutes, the way others dipped into swimming pools for similar amounts of time. Their perfection exhilarated him—the grim and mournful O'Brien; the psychotic but fascinating Ralph Meeker; and the black-and-white photography that showed roots in German expressionism but that became, in these instances, inexorably American—the urban streets at night, the millions of twisted tales played out on them.

He was watching Edmond O'Brien down the fatal glass of poison when the phone rang in his cabin. He swore and punched Freeze on the VCR remote control.

"Hello."

"I want to say this in a friendly way." The voice, sleek, theatrical, modulated, belonged to the sort of man who would spend a good deal of time catching his reflection in mirrors and windows.

"Say what in a friendly way?"

"I know you're doing a little snooping about."

"What gives you that impression?"

"I had a bite with Alicia Farris."

It was nice to be able to trust people, Tobin thought. He'd had the impression, while talking to Alicia, that they were friendly if not exactly friends. But apparently Alicia had reported right back to Todd Ames.

"I see."

"We should stick together, Tobin; the 'Celebrity Circle' people, I mean."

"I didn't know that we weren't."

"You're going around asking questions."

"You make that sound like some sort of betrayal."

Todd Ames's voice got very tight. "In a way, I consider it a betrayal." He paused. "There's the show to consider."

"Ah. The show."

"You're not very good with sarcasm."

"I guess I'm just sort of old-fashioned."

"And how would that be?"

"I'd just naturally assumed that three deaths took precedence over 'the show.'"

Another pause. "Did you like 'Celebrity Gardener?'"

"I beg your pardon?"

"Did you like that show?"

"Not much, no."

"You work very hard for twenty or thirty years and you nearly make it to the top and then—well, something unfortunate happens to you, and there you are one day . . . on 'Celebrity Gardener.' After you'd had your own network series and been on the cover of *TV Guide* and been interviewed countless times on 'ET' and . . . I think you know what I'm talking about."

"You're saying that you've all worked hard."

"Precisely."

"And that 'Celebrity Circle' is your one and only . . . blue chip stock, I suppose."

"Yes."

"And that it's been jeopardized."

"Badly so."

"And that I shouldn't be asking questions because that only casts more unfavorable light on the show."

"You're beginning to understand and I really appreciate that."

"I'm not unsympathetic, Todd."

"Thank you."

"Being a has-been is no easy life. I happen to be one."

"I don't really care for that implication. We're hardly has-been's."

"No, but you are almost totally dependent on 'Celebrity Circle' for your income and whatever prestige it gives you."

"It may interest you to know that Universal contacted my agent just before we sailed and that there's a pilot in the offing and—"

"So you'd give up your new position as host of 'Celebrity Circle' for the pilot?"

"Of course not. But . . ."

Tobin gathered himself and said, "A friend of mine tells me that on the night Ken Norris died, he threw a drink in your face. I wonder if you'd care to tell me why."

"Once this cruise is over, Tobin, you'll never work on 'Celebrity Circle' again. I can promise you that."

"And last night at dinner, Cassie McDowell stood up and slapped you. I wonder if you could shed any light on that for me."

"What the hell do you have against us, anyway?"

"Nothing, Todd, believe it or not. I just happen to take murder very seriously."

In books people are always chuckling. Tobin had

never been sure what that particular noise was actually supposed to sound like. But just then Todd Ames made a noise that Tobin could only classify as a "chuckle." It was an irritating sound. "You know, back in my theater days—I don't know if you knew that I worked with Kate Hepburn and Larry Olivier—anyway, back then I did a murder play and every night I'd come home, I'd find myself petrified to go into my apartment. Afraid."

But Tobin was still back on "Kate" and "Larry."

"I guess I'm not seeing the point, Todd," Tobin said.

"The point is that I don't like murder much, either. So I suppose I'd just as soon let the police handle all this when we get back to the States."

"Right," Tobin said, "and give the killer plenty of time to cover his or her tracks and get away." He paused. "You haven't answered my questions yet. Why did Ken throw a drink in your face and why did Cassie slap you?"

"Neither one of those questions is any of your business."

"Maybe I'll make them my business."

"We're a family," Todd Ames said. "We squabble like a family—but we've been a family ever since Day One of 'Celebrity Circle.' And we're going to amaze you with how close-knit we are."

"You're saying you won't cooperate with any investigation?"

"We have our reputations plus a show to protect, Tobin. You don't seem to understand that."

"I'm afraid I do understand, Todd, and only too well."

"You're being sarcastic again."

"I'm just trying to find out what's going on."

"Let's leave that to the authorities."

"There are lives at stake here."

"There's also a show at stake."

Tobin paused, seeing he was getting nowhere. Then, "I nearly forgot."

"Forgot what?"

"When Ken Norris threw a drink in your face, he told my friend, 'Todd's just sick of payday.' What did that mean?"

Tobin got the response he'd expected.

Todd Ames slammed down the phone.

22 3:12 P.M.

Dear Aberdeen,

You remember that real macho guy who used to be in that cop series, Kevin Anderson? Well, guess who's sleeping (snoring, actually, except mentioning that kind of spoils the effect of the mood I'm trying to create here) right next to me?

God, I can't believe it!

Right next to me!

Sleeping!

How it happened was we had two more murders on this boat—next time I go on a cruise ship, it's definitely going to be on a different line—and I went with Tobin (the TV critic you always said was cute even if he was short!) to check it out and then Tobin went to do something and—

Well, anyway, Kevin asked me if I wanted to go have a drink and I figured, you know, what could be the harm.

But he meant a drink in his room.

I wasn't real sure but then—you know how easily I can be influenced sometimes—he told me he'd had a small part in *Saturday Night Fever* and had actually gone drinking with John Travolta—and then that's what we got.

Ken and I, I mean—drunk.

And then next thing—

Well, he's sleeping right next to me.

(Back now. I had to go tinkle.) But I have to admit he's kind of weird, Kevin is. When he thought I was passed out, I heard him on the phone talking about this meeting the people on 'Celebrity Circle' were going to have—right in the middle of the night.

Then after he was gone, I got up and barfed and then I went back to bed, still trying to figure out why the 'Celebrity Circle' people would have a meeting that late and then I heard somebody come up to the door outside and I thought it might be the killer again so I scooched under the covers and waited and waited and waited and I really prayed (I was saying Hail Mary's, Aberdeen, and I'm not even Catholic) and then I heard this little swishing noise like under the door and I realized that somebody had pushed something under there and then I heard steps hurrying away down the corridor and when I finally got up to see what it was, I found this envelope and it was like weird-o-rama, Aberdeen, because inside was this really crummy Xerox copy of a picture of this little six-month-old baby. Who would send something like that.

I overheard Kevin tell Cassie in the bar that he'd gotten something yesterday, too—then this second letter. Really strange.

"What you writin', babe?"

"Oh, good morning, Kevin."

"Good morning. So what're you writing?"

"Just kind of like a note."

"A note."

"Well, more like a letter."

"A letter?"

"Yes."

"To who?"

"Aberdeen."

"Who's that?"

"This sort of heavy-set woman who has a mustache I work with at the insurance company."

He was bored instantly. "Oh."

"I was telling her about last night."

They were naked. It was the middle of the afternoon and they were still naked from the night before and needing showers and . . .

He reached over and kissed her right breast (the one whose nipple was about a quarter-inch longer than the other one, which really bugged her when she thought about it, and she thought about it more than you'd think) and said, "So you told her about us."

"Well."

"It's OK, babe."

"It is?"

"Sure."

He grinned. "First 'cause I'm good and I know I am and second because, well, it's just human nature to spread the news when you sleep with a celebrity."

"It is?"

He was propped up on one elbow now and deftly stroking her shoulder. With his hair mussed, and slightly in need of a shave, and enough chest hair to make a grizzly envious, he really looked hunky. Really.

"Sure. First month I was in Hollywood, I slept with the late Constance LaRue."

"Are you serious?"

"Right. I had just come out from a farm in South

Dakota and I was parking cars at what's now the Harlequin Dinner Theater and she spotted me."

"You mean spotted you for a movie or something?"

He grinned again. "Or something. Connie—Constance—she liked very young, very industrious men."

"But she played a nun in that musical with . . ." She shook her head. Boy, wait till she told Aberdeen about what Constance LaRue was really like.

"Have you ever been on Johnny Carson?" she asked.

"Couple of times."

"He as nice as he seems?"

"He's an asshole. He should've quit ten years ago. On top. That's the only way to go out." He paused. "That's how I left my series. On top."

Without thinking, Cindy said, "But wasn't your series canc—"

And then, seeing the glare in his eyes, she said, "Oh, that's right. You quit because you wanted to do movies."

"Right."

"I saw that one too. *The Fungoids.* It was really great."

"Writing wasn't all it could've been but it was a good vehicle for me. It went through the roof in South America so I went down there a few years and made a bundle. That's how I bought all those doughnut franchises I was tellin' you about last night."

"Oh, right." Actually, Cindy had tried to forget about the doughnut franchises because somehow they spoiled the effect.

Actors should act and when they weren't acting they should stand at picture windows and swish brandy around in snifters and let the crest on their smoking jackets kind of gleam in the shadows.

"I'm a morning man."

"Huh?" Cindy said. Her eyes had strayed to her

purse, where she'd stuck the envelope that had been pushed under his door. Ever since waking up, she'd been thinking of how she was going to tell him about the envelope.

Because it was definitely a problem.

How could she show him the envelope without explaining to him that in effect she'd been opening his mail?

"Couldn't we take a shower first?"

"Great idea. Together."

"No, I didn't mean . . ."

But he was kissing her, and even with morning mouth (his and hers alike) she forgot all about the envelope.

Twenty minutes later, she had at least six new things to tell Aberdeen about Kevin Anderson.

Seven if you counted what he showed her to do with the soap.

23 5:24 P.M.

By now of course Tobin was beginning to assume the worst. Not only had Cindy McBain gone off with Kevin Anderson but she had most definitely slept with him. All morning Tobin had been able to tell himself that maybe Anderson had gotten to first or maybe second or maybe even, after plying her with drinks, third base, but no home run stuff, no out-of-the-park routines. But, as Tobin knocked on her empty room several times, and then checked various lounges and eateries, and then walked the length of several decks never so much as glimpsing her—gradually he began to understand the real implication of what was going on here. And, ridiculous as it was, he felt betrayed and jealous. She hadn't made love to Tobin because she'd been so upset with Ken Norris's death. But the blond macho TV cop was apparently another matter.

Quite another matter, Tobin thought as he made his way along the middle deck into the sunlight and in the direction of the captain's cabin. He assumed that by now Dr. Devane had sobered up and that both he and the Captain had had time to go through the dead people's effects. Perhaps they'd learned something useful about Iris Graves and the man killed with her.

A deck tennis game was in progress as Tobin reached the unfettered sunlight. He was dressed in a white shirt and white ducks and white deck shoes without socks. His red hair was brilliant in the yellow light. He smiled as passengers waved in recognition, or pointed or whispered. He owed them courtesy. God knew they'd put up with him and his pontifications on the tube (he could still recall saying, in a spontaneous if obscure burst, that John Ford was "a racist but not a malicious one," and while *he* knew what he'd meant, nobody else had, as evidenced by the hundreds of letters comparing him to various Nazi figures, and KKK leaders) and he should be in return, and at the least, polite.

The blue water of the pool shimmered as if it were not quite real. Around the perimeter, on the tiles, lay any number of women who could fulfill the most exotic of Tobin's fantasies.

One of them, delightfully enough, even reached out and grasped his ankle.

"Not speaking?"

"Oh, hi," Tobin said.

"Did you finally get some sleep?"

"Finally. And you?"

She smiled. "Finally." Susan Richards was even better looking in the daylight wearing a one-piece white bathing suit, such suits invariably reminding him of Julie Adams in *The Creature From the Black Lagoon,* a seventh-grade spectacle so astonishing that he began to understand that the most exalted feeling on the planet, right next to godliness, was horniness. She wore sunglasses so black he could not even glimpse the shape of her eyes behind them. She smiled. "But my wrinkles were still there, this morning."

"Wrinkles?"

"Around my eyes and mouth. My agent wants me to pay a little visit to my friendly neighborhood plastic surgeon because I got turned down for a role two months ago. Because of my age."

"You're beautiful, Susan, and you know it."

She dismissed his compliment with a graceful hand. "Twenty-two lines in a Raquel Welch mini-series. I was supposed to be her younger sister. But the casting director said I was too old." She laughed but there was a chilly sadness in her voice. "Oh, he didn't say it quite that way, of course. I think he said, 'Raquel and you are too much alike. It might confuse the audience.'" She paused then. "We had a meeting."

"Who had a meeting?"

"The regulars on 'Celebrity Circle.'"

"Oh?"

"Yes, and Todd said that you think one of us is the killer. Is that right?"

He shrugged. "I don't know who else it could be."

Her beautiful mouth became ironic. "Does that include me?"

"Well . . ."

"You're cute when you're trying to be evasive." She put out a hand to be helped up. He thought of holding this same hand last night. The darkness seemed impossible now that yellow day burned the deck.

As she stood up, she grabbed a black leather Gucci casual bag and a tiny framed black-and-white photograph of a little girl. He was about to ask her about the girl when Jere Farris strolled by and said, "Coming to the costume party tonight?" and then went on without waiting for an answer.

"Well," Susan Richards said, "are you?"

"I suppose."

"You sound delighted."

"It's the idea of dressing up in funny clothes, I guess.

I've never been able to figure out why adults like to do that."

She leaned in and kissed him on the cheek, and he thought of last night again, now so idyllic in memory, and she laughed like wind chimes and said, "Who said we're adults, Tobin?"

24

6:13 P.M.

"Sanderson was a private detective."

"From an agency?"

"Agency?"

"Yes," Tobin said, "a detective agency. Like Pinkerton's."

The captain shook his head. "Not from the looks of this brochure. I'd say he was strictly free-lance and not exactly running an empire, either."

He handed Tobin a two-color trifold brochure. The paper was rough to the touch and you could see where the ink had smudged in the printing. The outer panel said, CONFIDENTIAL INVESTIGATIONS OUR SPECIALTY.

"Pretty much what you'd expect," Captain Hackett said as Tobin opened up the flap and looked inside.

There were several photographs of Everett Sanderson, all of them taken when he was much younger. In one photo he wore navy whites; in another, a dark police uniform; in a third (and the most recent) he appeared as he had aboard this cruise ship, a chunky, sixtyish man in a conservative western suit with a white Stetson, string tie, and bulldoglike jowls. The copy beneath these photos referred to the fact that Everett Sanderson had served first his country, then his city, and now, on a for-hire basis, he was serving the public.

"Simpson, Kentucky," Captain Hackett said.

They sat in his office. Sunlight streamed through their whiskey glasses, giving the liquid a golden gleam, as the ceiling fan chopped briskly at stale air. The captain explained that the Coast Guard would be sending investigators within thirty-six hours.

"That mean anything to you?" Tobin said.

"No. I was hoping it meant something to you."

Tobin smiled. "Afraid not. But there is something that would mean something to me."

"What's that?"

"What you and the doctor checked Cindy McBain for the other morning."

"I guess you're on our side now."

"Is that an answer?"

The captain sighed. "We found blood." The captain paused.

"Why didn't you tell me?"

"We weren't quite sure you could keep a secret." He frowned. "I'm sorry, Tobin."

"Tell me about the blood."

"There was plenty of it. He'd been stabbed."

"A second blood type on the rug. We think that the killer must have cut him or herself while stabbing Ken Norris. So we were checking Miss McBain's hands and arms for any cut marks."

"You didn't find any."

"Correct." He hesitated. Cleared his throat softly. "But we did find somebody with exactly the sort of cut marks we would have expected."

"You did?"

"Yes. Miss Graves."

"The dead woman?"

"Right. And, in her belongings, we also found a notebook—a sort of journal, actually. She wrote about going into Miss McBain's room—after following Ken Norris all night. But she didn't cut herself on the knife. She cut herself on a piece of a lamp that had been knocked over and shattered. That's what she said in her journal and that squares with what we found at the scene." Now it was his turn to smile. "She was also the mysterious figure in the trenchcoat and snap-brim hat your friend McBain kept going on about."

"Why the hell was she following Norris?"

"Story, presumably." He leaned leftward, opened a drawer, and withdrew the small brown leather notebook Alicia Farris and Iris Graves had been struggling over the day of Iris's death. "She has a lot of rambling notes in here. I spent most of last night sipping sherry and looking through them. Care to take the notebook and see what you can come up with?"

"Sure."

The captain said, "They're hiding something."

"Who?"

"The 'Celebrity Circle' bunch. You'll see that very clearly when you start reading the notebook there. Something binds them together—but I'm not sure what."

"You heard about Cassie McDowell slapping Todd Ames last night?"

"Yes."

"Whatever binds them together seems to be coming apart."

"That's my impression too." He glanced out the porthole. "Some days I wish I would have been a Greyhound driver." He poured some brandy from his cut-glass snifter. "My daughter from Oak Park was supposed to bring her children on this cruise. Thank Christ one of my granddaughters came down with the measles." He turned back to Tobin. "I don't have any idea what Sanderson was doing on this trip but I suspect he was working with her."

"With Iris Graves?"

"Isn't it likely?"

Tobin considered. Then, "She worked for *Snoop*. It's a publication that probably hires dozens of private investigators. I suppose they could have been working on a story together."

"I keep thinking back to when they were all in the party room—when I told them about Norris's death."

"Their reaction, you mean?"

"They reminded me of wartime. I was in Korea. I got that way—about death, I mean." He glanced out the porthole again. A tattered golden cloud dragged by. "The first death I ever saw—well, it was a corporal and of course I couldn't let the other fellows see me cry. But that night in my tent . . ." His jaw locked as he returned his gaze to Tobin. "I guess I can understand servicemen getting that callous about death—but why would celebrities?"

Tobin sighed. "To be fair to them, they're fighting their own war; against age and the loss of their looks, against constant competition, and against just sheer luck. There are so many people who want to make it in Hollywood. An environment like that doesn't exactly spawn wonderful people."

"You don't seem like that."

Tobin laughed. "But I am. Deep down. When my partner was murdered I didn't think of anything except clearing my name. It was six months before it hit me. I was walking past a theater where we used to go when we were young and poor and where they always played black-and-whites from the forties. And then I realized that the only thing that was keeping my partner alive was my memory of him—and what we'd looked like then, and what we'd wanted to be, and how we'd tried to be cool and impress girls—and here were all these memories and I had to keep them alive be-

≈ *125*

cause that was the only way to keep him alive. That corner had been there nearly a hundred years and hundreds of thousands of people had passed by and fashions had changed and wars had come and gone and everything that had seemed so important had vanished utterly, without a trace, but in my brain I had a memory of two young men and what that corner had been like in the summer of 1964 when Barry Goldwater was running for president and when the Beatles were popular and when the girl I was dating would cry every time we made love because she was convinced it was 'wrong.' All those things had happened and when I die nobody will know about those things anymore, at least not in the way I knew about them, the way we each know things differently, and so all I can do for my partner is remember him. You understand?"

"Of course."

"But I don't feel that when most people die. Not the older I get, anyway. Most deaths just make me worry about my own mortality—I'm just selfish." He held up his glass and said, "So thanks for the compliment, Captain, but I'm afraid it's undeserved. I didn't give a damn when Norris died, either."

"But you weren't supposed to be his friend. They were." He nodded to the notebook. "She's got several references in there to each of them but they don't make any sense—they're just like the rest of the notebook."

"Newspaper people develop their own kind of shorthand the way court stenographers sometimes do. Maybe that's all it is."

"Maybe." Then he reached behind him and hefted a cardboard box. "Here are Sanderson's things. Want a look at them? My security people have been through them, cataloged everything for when we turn it all over to the Coast Guard."

"I caught him eavesdropping on the party room that night. Did I tell you that?"

"No."

Tobin nodded. "He probably knew who killed Norris and why and so did Iris Graves."

Captain Hackett laughed. "Well, if they left any clues for us, I hope you have better luck finding them than I did." Then he glanced at his watch. "Afraid I've got a meeting, Tobin." He pushed the cardboard box across the desk. "Appreciate the help."

25 6:48 P.M.

"Did you ever sleep with somebody and regret it?"

Nothing.

"Did you ever sleep with somebody when it was really somebody else you really wanted to sleep with?"

Nada.

"Did you ever sleep with somebody and all the time pretend it was really somebody else you were sleeping with?"

Tobin said to Cindy McBain, "Why don't you just shut up?"

"It was only because I was drunk."

"Right."

She thought a moment. "And, well, I guess because of Aberdeen."

What could he say?

"Well, aren't you going to ask why it was because of Aberdeen?"

"No."

"C'mon, Tobin. Just ask me."

"I said no."

"Then I'll tell you."

He did something with his fingers then.

"Boy, I wish you could see how childish you look. You really do. Your fingers in your ears."

Then she reached up and took one finger out of his ear and then she whispered something incredible in it and then she took the other finger out of the other ear and whispered something equally incredible into that one. She smelled of perfume and soft sweet female flesh and real blond hair.

Then she put her mouth on his and pushed him gently back onto the bed in his cabin.

Things happened quickly after that.

"It was a good lesson for me."

"Right."

"Well, it was. God, Tobin, I'm glad I'm not as cynical as you."

"If it was such a good lesson, what did you learn?"

"Well . . ."

There was silence.

Tobin said, "So what did you learn?"

"I learned about sincerity."

"You sound like a contestant on Miss America."

"That was a cheap remark."

"Yes, it was and I apologize."

"You're still jealous and you're still angry."

"Yes, I am." Then, "So you learned about sincerity and what else?"

"I learned I shouldn't do things just to impress other people."

"So you're never going to tell anybody that you slept with Kevin Anderson, famous TV star?"

"Well . . ."

"Well, what?"

"Well, only certain people."

"Such as Aberdeen."

"Yes, such as Aberdeen. If she wasn't so fat and she didn't have that mustache, then she wouldn't have to live—what's that word?"

"Vicariously."

"Right. She wouldn't have to live vicariously through me."

"So in a very real sense, the only reason you slept with him was for her sake."

"It does make for a more interesting letter."

"Am I going to be in your letter?"

"Do you want to be in my letter?"

"Only if it's in the most flattering terms."

She giggled. "Do you want me to lie?"

When she giggled, he started liking her again, and when he started liking her again he started getting mad at Kevin Anderson for what he'd done to her.

Because sitting there, luxuriant of flesh and wonderful of face, Cindy McBain, Kansas City secretary and purveyor of second-hand thrills to the mountainous Aberdeen, sported a black eye courtesy of Kevin Anderson's fist.

"So tell me again why he hit you?"

"Because the envelope fell out of my purse."

"And it was a Xerox of a small child's picture?"

"Huh-uh. And when he saw it he just went crazy. He really did. He started accusing me of meddling in his affairs and he said I hadn't had any right to open the envelope and he said if I didn't watch what I was doing I was going to wind up dead like those three other people—and then he just hit me." She paused. "Jim-the-Cowboy hit me once. He said in Montana women are hit all the time."

"Jim-the-Cowboy?"

"I went to a rodeo once and . . . Well, I wouldn't want you to get the wrong idea."

"God forbid."

"You think it had anything to do with the killings? The envelope, I mean?"

"I'm wondering."

Tobin eyed the cardboard box and the brown leather notebook. He'd been back in his room only five minutes when the shamed Cindy McBain had applied supplicant knuckles to his door. He hadn't had a chance to examine any of the things Captain Hackett had given to him and now, in light of Cindy's information about the envelope slid under Kevin Anderson's door, he was very curious.

"Why don't you take a nap?"

"I was hoping you'd say that. Scooch over."

"No," Tobin said. "I mean, in your room. Then I'll pick you up for dinner and the costume party. Around eight or so—all right?"

"You want to get rid of me, don't you?"

He kissed her softly on the mouth—liking her more and more, her odd mix of innocence and corruption—and said, "Exactly."

≈ *131*

26

Iris Graves must have been lauded by all her grade school teachers for her penmanship. She'd written in a clear, painstaking hand that was nearly beautiful to look at. Toward the front of the book were other stories she was working on, including a rock star who was apparently contemplating a sex change operation or who was, in fact, the gender opposite of the one fans assumed—Iris's ambiguity was at its height here—and then a tale about a senator seeing a starlet and various other juicy but ultimately banal bits. Unfortunately, the words referring to the "Celebrity Circle" group were the most obscure of all.

Oh, there were plenty of teasers scattered throughout the section headed "Celebrity Circle."

Jere Farris end/Cassie McDowell up/Ken Norris rich (see banker Beverly Hills)/Susan Richards "belle"

Obviously, the key words were "end" and "up" and "banker Beverly Hills" and "belle" but what the hell could they possibly mean to anybody but Iris Graves?

He paused for a time, rubbing his eyes, cat-lazy, and viewed a few frames of *New York Ripper,* about which nothing further needed to be said. It was one of those flicks where the title pretty much wrote your review for you, especially after you saw the first thirty seconds in which a gigantic knife appeared to plunge downward into a gigantic breast.

Yessir.

So he went back to his reading, forming a picture of beautiful, red-haired Iris as his eyes scanned the pages. She'd been a regal one, Iris had, and he'd wondered how she'd ever wound up working for a cheesy rag like *Snoop*.

Then near the end of the journal he found it—a single word.

"Payday."

Actually, it was contained in a sentence that went: "Wonder how Ken Norris' loyal fans will appreciate his payday? Ask BV banker how long been going on."

BV presumably meant Beverly Hills again.

But what the hell was "payday" all about?

By the time he got to unloading the cardboard box of items belonging to Everett Sanderson, Tobin had begun to feel something like a grave robber. He recalled moving into an apartment near Central Park where the previous occupant, a painter, had died of a heart attack on the living room floor. One day, tucked in the back of a closet, Tobin had found a packet of letters from the painter to his daughter, and much as he'd been moved by what he read, Tobin had always felt obscene about it, as if he'd window-peeked or something.

He had something of the same feeling as he lifted things from the box. There was a Louis L'Amour paperback western, a package of Chesterfield cigarettes unopened, a Sony cartridge tape recorder, a few dozen of the brochures Captain Hackett had shown him, a .38 Smith and Wesson, a wallet filled with pictures of Sanderson's grandchildren and a very faded photo of Sanderson standing in front of a trailer with another man who was holding an infant lovingly in his arms; beside him was the body of a woman. Sanderson, or somebody, had taken a Magic Marker and obliterated her face. The violence of this intrigued Tobin. He slipped the photo from its cellophane and then clipped on his bed lamp and looked at it more carefully. He could see nothing of her face beyond the Magic Marker. She wore a tie-dyed shirt and he could see a peace symbol painted on the shabby house trailer behind them so he assumed the photograph dated back to the mid-to-late sixties. Sanderson, standing on the far right of the photograph, looked somber.

Tobin took the photograph to the bathroom. He wet Kleenex, then gently daubed the soaked paper over the Magic Marker. But the black ink was indelible. He could not see the face of the woman.

After a quick glance at the TV—"the New York Ripper" was slashing his sixteenth or seventeenth victim—Tobin picked up the wallet and started going through the money compartment. There was $400 in various denominations and then three folded-up, yellowed newspaper clippings.

The first clipping made him smile. "Sanderson Bowls Perfect Game," and then a brief account of how a Louisville, Kentucky, policeman had rolled 300 in a policeman's league bowling tournament. The story brought the man alive to Tobin and for the first time he found himself wondering about Sanderson as a human being—the way, he supposed, archaeologists wondered about Egyptians on the site of digs. What had made Sanderson happy or sad? What had he liked to watch on TV? What failures had he endured and triumphs enjoyed (aside from that one perfect bowling game)?

The next two clippings were more like Iris Graves's notes—virtually meaningless because they had no context.

HARBURT MAN PERISHES
IN TRAILER FIRE

Twenty-six-year-old William K. Kelly was found burned to death yesterday in his house trailer on Puckett Road.

Preliminary investigation indicates that Kelly fell asleep with a cigarette in his hand. Fire authorities believe the blaze started in a couch on which Kelly slept.

The second clipping read:

SANDY CUMMINGS WINS
MISS INDIANA

Sandy Cummings, a twenty-three-year-old doctor's receptionist from Muncie, was crowned Miss Indiana last night in an event that was telecast statewide for the first time.

The clipping went on to detail runners-up and all the usual hype put forth by officials, one of whom said, "This shows you that not all our young people are out hurling rocks and picketing."

Tobin had the sense that the clipping—like the photo—dated from the sixties.

But what the hell did it mean?

The next tape Tobin watched was a Roger Corman movie called *The Man With the X-Ray Eyes*, a very good remake of the Ray Milland original.

He was about halfway through it—real time; no fast forward with a film like this—when Don Rickles (in what was apparently his movie debut) tells the Milland character that he knows all about him and could turn him in for a reward.

It was that last word, "reward," that gave Tobin the idea.

He called collect.

When you call New York from somewhere in the middle of the Pacific Ocean, you tend to run up a bill rather quickly.

He asked for the entertainment editor and just hoped that the man or woman—Tobin was not a reader of the rag and so had no idea which—would recognize Tobin's name from his various TV appearances.

A receptionist put the operator through to a second person and then a male voice said, "Conroy."

"I have a collect call from a man who says he's Tobin, the TV critic. Will you accept charges? He's calling from aboard a cruise ship."

"Is this a gag?"

The operator sounded irritated. "I'm too busy for gags, sir." Ma Bell might have learned to grovel for business following deregulation, but she had yet to get herself a sense of humor.

"Is this really Tobin?" Conroy said.

"It's really Tobin," Tobin said.

"You are not permitted to speak, sir," the operator said, "until Mr. Conroy accepts the charges."

"All right, for God's sake, I accept the charges." When the woman rang off, Conroy said, "Bitch." Then, "So what can I do for you, Tobin?"

"I'm on the same cruise ship where Iris Graves was murdered."

"Say, that's right. Poor Iris. She was one hell of a

woman—and I don't mean just looks-wise, either. Good reporter."

"That's one of the things I wanted to ask you about."

"What?"

"What she was working on."

"Can't tell you because I don't know and wouldn't tell you if I did."

"You still pay $10,000 for your lead story?"

"Yep. They can call us what they want but they can't say we don't pay our writers."

"Writers" was stretching it where *Snoop* was concerned. Generally, *Snoop* got its stuff from waiters, parking lot attendants, and hospital officials—its Liberace AIDS story had been leaked by an orderly, for example—and then one of the staffers just "worked it up," doing a little what they liked to call "enhancing" along the way.

Other less genteel folks called it lying.

Tobin couldn't resist. "Do you pay twice as much if the story happens to be true?"

Conroy surprised him by laughing. "Everybody I know who knows you says you're an asshole and, boy, they're right."

"Thanks."

"So in other words you've got a story you want to sell?"

"Well, I can't write the story without some help from you but if you go along, I think I can piece together something you'd really like."

"You think you can find out who killed Norris as well as Iris and this guy Sanderson?"

"Yes."

"You got any hunches right now?"

"Not right now. But speaking of Sanderson—that would be my first question."

"So we're going to make a deal?"

Tobin knew there was a special place in hell for people who worked with *Snoop* but he also knew that $10,000 was the equivalent of five appearances on "Celebrity Gardener."

"Just one thing," Tobin said.

"Way ahead of you. You want me to absolutely guarantee you your anonymity."

"Right."

"Because you'd be ashamed to be associated with a rag like ours."

"Right."

"But you'd be more than happy to take our money."

"Right."

"What a hypocrite."

"Were they working together?"

"Iris and Sanderson?"

"Yes."

"No."

"You're sure?"

"I talked to her the day she died. She said she was getting close to finishing her story but that there might be an even bigger one because of Sanderson."

"And that's all she said?"

"Right."

"So what was her story?"

"I'm not sure."

"I thought we were supposed to be cooperating."

"Actually, it's true. I was on vacation and she suddenly took off on this cruise. All she told me was that she was going to expose a very big scandal about 'Celebrity Circle.'"

"And that's all?"

"That's all. She had this thing—she hated talking

about stories before they were finished. Bad luck. I know a lot of fiction writers who are like that."

"She use the word 'payday?'"

"Huh-uh."

"She say anything about any of the panelists on the show?"

"I told you, she didn't like to talk about the story."

"You want to give me your phone credit card?"

"You serious?"

"Of course I'm serious. I'm going to have to reconstruct what Iris was working on and since I'm in the middle of the Pacific, the only way I can do that is with phone calls."

"I thought you TV guys made a lot of money."

"Not when you do 'Celebrity Fitness' and stuff like that."

"You need the money, huh?"

"To be honest, yes."

Conroy said, "Then let's make it I approve the phone tab up to two grand and I pay you eight grand if the story goes in as our lead."

"I'm paying for my own phone calls?"

"Two grand's more money than you had five minutes ago, Tobin."

Tobin swore.

"And we won't use your name. I promise you."

Tobin said, "Deal."

27

8:41 P.M.

"You're not going to the costume party?" Cassie McDowell said.

"I just haven't come up with a costume yet."

"You've only got about an hour or so before dinner." She herself was ready to go as Bo Peep, complete with bonnet and petticoats and big, clunky children's-book shoes. "You like it?"

"You going to invite me in?"

"Really, I need some positive reinforcement. Now, do you like it or not?"

"It's cute. Now, are you going to invite me in?"

He was in the corridor outside her door. Passengers got up in rigs ranging from Donald Duck to Darth Vader squeezed by. He felt foolish standing out there, as if they all knew that she wouldn't let him in.

"What do you want?"

"Just to talk."

"About what?"

Any notion he'd had that she'd been interested in him in any personal way was long gone. He stood there in jeans and his I SURVIVED THE TEXAS CHAINSAW MASSACRE II T-shirt and said, "It's just a friendly visit."

"Right."

She turned just so in the light from her cabin, and he could see how quickly her face was aging and there was something sad about it, because her youth was all she'd had on "McKinley High, USA." No talent; not even animal charm. Just that cuteness, and now it was resisting the skin lotion she smelled of, now it was resisting everything she put up against the inevitable.

"We didn't kill anybody—none of us."

"I was just curious," Tobin said, "why you slapped Todd in the face last night."

"Strain, and nothing more. I'm not exactly used to people being murdered. I was just reacting to the strain was all."

"Sanderson, the private detective who was killed, had something in his belongings that made me very curious."

She looked surprised. "You have his belongings?"

"Yes."

"How'd you get them?"

"Captain Hackett."

"Isn't that cozy?" From the pocket on her dress she took a package of Salem Lights and lit one. "I really don't have time for this. We're supposed to have an open bar for the passengers up on the Promenade deck in ten minutes. I wouldn't expect you to lower yourself for anything like that." She seemed agitated—and had been ever since he mentioned Sanderson's belongings.

"I didn't know you'd won a beauty contest in Indiana."

"What?"

"A beauty contest in Indiana."

"I never have been in Indiana. I was born and raised in Culver City. The only thing I like about the Midwest is that it's so far away I never have to go there."

"You're sure?"

"You think I don't remember where I live?"

"Did you ever live in a trailer?"

"No. And I'm sick of your questions."

She looked sad then, and silly, standing there in her costume and he felt sorry for her. He wondered if she knew how sad and silly she looked. She was one of those doggedly happy people whom you secretly suspect are always miserable.

Except now she wasn't even doggedly happy. She wasn't happy at all.

"Does the word 'payday' mean anything to you?"

"No." But she said it far too quickly.

"Ken Norris used that word."

"I wouldn't know."

"When you slapped Todd you screamed at him that you were all glad Ken was dead."

"I was drunk."

"But you said it."

"So?"

"Why did you all hate him?"

"You didn't like him yourself. I saw how you watched him."

"But I didn't hate him."

She adjusted her Bo Peep bonnet. "I need to finish getting ready, Tobin. I can't say I've enjoyed this conversation."

Tobin said, "You wouldn't know where Ken Norris did his banking by any chance, would you?"

And he saw it then—panic on her face. He had no idea why the reference would have rattled her but obviously it had.

"Just get out of here," she said.

She closed the door before he could say anything else.

Ten minutes later he found the producer, Jere Farris, in one of the small lounges.

There was a piano player in a red lamé dinner jacket

struggling with a Nat King Cole song. It was very dark and in the darkness tiny red candles burned inside red glass globes. The seats were leather. They made a squishing sound when you sat in them.

Jere Farris looked relaxed for the first time in the two weeks Tobin had known him. It was due in large measure to the fact Jere Farris was potzed. Or at least seriously working toward such.

Farris wore a white golf shirt with a sweater tied rakishly around his neck. A massive Rolex watch rode his slender wrist, diamonds glittered in the globe light each time he took a drink. He smoked a cigarette with a ferocity that was disarming in these days of anti-smoking campaigns everywhere you looked. But even here, away from the frenzy, there was an air of petulance and prissiness about him. He was not the sort of man Tobin liked much, self-absorbed and waspish, unwilling to acknowledge in any way that you might have griefs just as he had griefs.

Tobin said, "Mind if I sit down?"

"Seems you already have."

"Mind if I order a drink?"

"As long as you don't expect me to pay for it."

Tobin said, "I'm now officially a pariah?"

Farris jabbed out his cigarette. "I don't know what the hell you think you're doing."

"Trying to find out what's going on. In case you forgot, three people have been killed."

"Yes, and they've ruined the entire voyage. This was supposed to be nothing but good publicity."

Tobin thought of Captain Hackett's remark about the callousness of show-biz people. "You all wanted Ken Norris dead."

"You can prove that?"

"Not at the moment but Iris Graves, the reporter

who was killed, was working on it." He paused. "I've been going through her things."

Farris reacted just as Cassie McDowell had. With surprise. "How'd you get her things?"

"Captain Hackett asked me to go through her belongings—and Sanderson's, the detective's."

Farris sat back in his chair. He looked defeated. "I don't suppose you give a damn that you're ruining our livelihoods. I mean, I really don't look forward to directing local news. This show is my last best shot. I'm forty years old."

Tobin calculated the effect of his words and said, "Do you happen to know where Ken Norris banked in Beverly Hills?"

And there it was. The same sort of glare he'd received from Cassie. But Farris was more skillful at recovering. "Now how would you expect me to know that?"

"The night he was killed you were—where?"

He sipped his drink. "You think you're a coy one, don't you, Tobin?"

"Meaning?"

"Meaning I know you and Joanna have discussed me. Joanna told me." He paused. "Joanna and I were together in her cabin."

"She'll swear to that?"

A tiny smile came on to his face. "She'll swear to anything I ask her to. She happens to love me."

He sounded like the second lead in a bad movie of a D. H. Lawrence book.

"You've got a nice wife, Farris. You should remember that."

"Next time I need advice about my love life, I'll be sure to write you a letter." He grinned with a great deal of malice. "I mean, you're so successful with women. You've been chasing Cindy McBain—and Kevin Anderson catches her."

He continued to grin as Tobin stood up, nodded, and walked away.

For all the unpleasantness, Tobin had achieved his purpose.

He'd now told two members of the "Celebrity Circle" group that the personal effects of Iris Graves and Everett Sanderson could be found in his cabin. They would inevitably tell all the others.

Now all Tobin had to do was wait and see who showed up to steal the stuff.

28

9:10 P.M.

He'd learned years ago to attend all costume parties as the Burglar.

Oh, people complained of course, and said he was a spoilsport and never got in the fun of anything. And that was, he supposed, true enough, having spent his earlier years as a rather public drunkard (lots of fistfights, most of which he lost) and would-be provocateur (years of boring people to death with his attacks on Godard, whom, he'd discovered one sober day, not many people liked much anyway). People now had the well-deserved impression that he could be at least a bit of a jerk about anything social, like a little boy who didn't want to get dressed up for his cousin's birthday party.

So the Burglar was perfect because while all these other people were making utter fools of themselves gotten up as Scaramouche and Donald Duck and Marie Antoinette, Tobin simply wore whatever sportcoat felt comfortable, slacks, a shirt and tie, and the simple Burglar mask—and *voilà!*—he was instantly transformed into the perfect costume party attendee.

"That's really kind of a mean thing to do," Cindy McBain said when he stopped by her cabin to pick her up. She wore a black-and-white nun's habit, the penguin-type, right down to the thunderous black oxfords. She was excitingly erotic, making Tobin wonder if he'd had a long-repressed desire to hump the nuns of his schoolboy youth. She'd worked wonders with makeup on her black eye.

"Why is it mean?"

"Because you're supposed to get in the spirit of the thing and all that and you've just got that crummy little mask on."

"Crummy little mask?"

"That really sucks, Tobin," Cindy said.

"Talk about not getting in the spirit," he said, as she bent over and locked the door of her cabin.

She stood up straight. "You're the one who's not in the spirit. I'm *right* in the spirit."

"You think real nuns use the word 'sucks'?"

Everybody was drunk.

Not just intoxicated, not just tipsy, not just sauced but rather glass-smashing, ass-pinching, bellow-resounding drunk.

And Tobin felt immediately caught up in it—the noise, the sweat, the confusion, the white flash of breast, the nylon flash of thigh—he wished he could abstract it all into one gigantic swimming pool and dive into the center of it.

The dinner and party spilled out of the restaurant and all over the deck. Waiters and stewards and waitresses toadied and simpered and cursed; insurance salesmen giggled. The deck was lined with tables, overwhelmed with food—steak and fish and poultry of every kind—and even the band inside onstage seemed caught up in the moment and actually managed to stay on key and hold their Vegas horseshit ("You know, there are a few cynics who think our Tribute to America segment isn't sincere, but let's have a round of applause to show 'em what we really think of our country, all right?") to a minimum.

Cindy, whose costume was particularly teasing to those men who'd been fortunate enough to catch her sunbathing, clutched his arm and said, "Can we eat with . . . them?"

"'Them?'"

"You know."

"Ah. 'Them.' Celebrities."

"It'd be nice. It really would."

"Even though at least one of 'them' is a killer."

"But eating with regular people'll be just . . . dull."

"And"—he smiled—"eating with regular people doesn't make for very exciting letters to Aberdeen."

"Not unless somebody choked on his food or something."

So they went inside and took their rightful place—being on "Celebrity Handyman" had to be worth some goddamn thing—at the table near the bandstand where a bunch of people who used to have network TV series sat.

It took some time for Tobin to recognize who was what but after a few drinks everything came clear.

Jere Farris, the producer, was dressed up as a cowboy; Alicia Farris was dressed up as Calamity Jane; Todd Ames, the new host, was Robin Hood and his wife, Beth, was a mermaid; Cassie McDowell was Bo Peep; Susan Richards was a hooker in a slit skirt and bountiful white peasant blouse; and Kevin Anderson was Tarzan. Everybody on the celebrity dais sat in a semicircle, just as they did on the "Celebrity Circle" set.

Only Anderson seemed even remotely happy to see Tobin and Cindy, and Anderson was interested only in Cindy. He looked as if he regretted throwing her out and blacking her eye this morning. Her nun's habit really did stir you up.

Tobin was about to start his third drink when he saw Joanna Howard sit down at a table out with the civilians. She was dressed up as Amelia Earhart—leather flying cap, leather jacket, fancy white trailing scarf—and she looked, in a stark way, lovely. She also looked, as always, lost.

"Poor kid," Tobin said, feeling his booze more than he'd imagined—or hoped—he would. Then he told Cindy all about Joanna's wretched love life.

Cindy nodded. "She reminds me of Aberdeen. Only skinnier."

"We should invite her up here to sit with us."

"Yes, we should." He was surprised to hear her slosh her words, as he was sloshing his.

He stood up—wobbly now—put his two pinkie fingers in his teeth, and whistled. Or tried to. About halfway through, he recalled that he didn't know *how* to whistle. It was just one of many reasons he'd felt inferior to all the other boys growing up. That and being slightly shorter than every kid's little brother.

So he did what seemed natural, at the moment anyway. He stood up and shouted, "Hey, Joanna!"

She was embarrassed by the attention.

Tobin persisted. "Hey, come on up here!"

So she came up, obviously just to keep him quiet.

"Quite a crowd, isn't it?" Joanna said, having to raise her voice to be heard above the drunken din. She was obviously uncomfortable raising her voice.

"You don't have a date, do you?" Cindy said. She made it sound as if Joanna had just had her arm amputated.

Joanna's eyes shifted miserably to Jere Farris, bombed and swinging a champagne glass around, spilling some on his spangly Grand Ole Opry cowboy clothes.

"No," she said.

"Then you get right up here and sit with us," Cindy said grandly, and started patting the empty chair next to her as if Joanna were a poodle who knew when to jump up on her mistress's lap.

"Oh," Joanna said, obviously about to protest.

"You come on now," Cindy McBain said. "I'm a nun and you're supposed to obey me." She giggled.

"Well," Joanna said, her eyes once again hooking forlornly on Jere's face. "Well, I guess it would be all right."

Three drinks later, Cindy, who held her liquor as well as any other horny fourteen-year-old junior-high girl said, "Tobin tells me you're in love with Jere Farris."

Which of course got Tobin one of those ten-thou-sand-daggers-in-your-heart glances from Joanna.

"I . . . I care for Jere."

Cindy patted her hand. "As soon as Tobin goes tin-kle, I'll tell you all about married men."

Tobin was about to protest when he felt Alicia Farris's glare on him. She obviously did not care to have her husband's mistress sitting at the same table and Tobin really didn't blame her. He'd been drunk enough that he'd forgotten all about the impropriety of asking Joanna up here.

The lounge boys left the stage to far too much ap-plause, replaced by a dance combo that turned "When Sunny Gets Blue" into a foxtrot.

The dancing began with confetti and streamers drift-ing from the ceiling.

Tobin turned to ask Cindy to dance but he saw that

she was deep in conversation with Joanna. "I've always had a simple rule about married men. If they don't give you a gift every month that's worth at least a thousand dollars, then you're really wasting your time."

Susan Richards must have seen Tobin's dilemma because she walked around the celebrity dais and came over to him. "Would you like to dance?"

"You're about three inches taller than me."

She smiled her wonderful smile. "You can stand on my feet."

The band played "Fly Me to the Moon" and they danced.

She smelled luxuriantly of perfume and herself and he held her tighter than was necessary but she didn't seem to mind, indeed laid her long fingers gently on the back of his neck as they moved through the melancholy darkness of the dance floor, the feeling like that of a New Year's Eve bash, hilarity and a certain sadness at the same time.

Then she startled him by leaning down (she was actually closer to five inches taller in her hooker heels) and brushing her mouth against his.

He came alive in a way that was almost painful, yet was also a wonderful experience for a forty-two-year-old sot who had recently begun worrying not about the quantity of his erections but the quality.

"My God," he said.

"I'm drunk."

"So am I."

"I only do this sometimes. I'm really not promiscuous."

"Neither am I," he said, "though it's not for want of trying."

She smiled. "'The maid who laughs is half taken.'"

"Fifteenth century, I believe."

"Something like that. But it's true. I like your jokes on the set. Everybody else is so concerned about the show. But you—"

She touched her mouth to his again.

He felt transported back to 1958 and the St. Michael's gym. He was moving as one about the floor with Mary Sue O'Hallahan. He knew she knew he had an erection that threatened to cause him a heart attack. He wondered if she minded. That had always been the big mystery in those days—did girls actually *want* you to get erections or did they just sort of put up with it when you did?

All these long years later, he was getting his answer.

"My cabin or yours?" she said easily.

And then he happened to glance over her shoulder—actually through her armpit, his level of vision not reaching her shoulder—and saw Todd Ames in his Robin Hood getup start to leave the celebrity dais.

Tobin assumed he was going one of two places. To the biffy or to Tobin's cabin.

Tobin would lay even money on the latter.

"Could we," he said miserably, "meet a little later?"

Pressed against him, and breathless as he, she said, "Later? Tobin, are you crazy?"

"I know. And I'm sorry. But . . ."

She stared at him with her overly made-up eyes (wasn't there a hooker someplace on God's own planet who didn't wear any makeup at all). With a quiet air of disbelief in her voice, she said, "You having some problems?"

"No."

"I mean, we don't have to jump on top of each other. Sometimes men your age—well, I love necking myself. It's like high school again."

Wretchedly, he watched Todd Ames leave the restaurant.

And all he could do was break and run.

"Tobin!" she shouted. "Tobin! You get back here!"

But by now Ames had vanished and Tobin was worried that he wouldn't be able to beat him back to his cabin.

He had to climb three flights of stairs and run down what seemed endless miles of corridor. He was sweating and panting and just about ready to barf when he reached his cabin door.

He pushed his ear to the wood and listened.

Party sounds floated up from below; a sky gorgeous with summer stars spread with radiant beauty round the entire world.

From inside, nothing.

Quickly, he inserted his key and ducked into his cabin.

29 10:21 P.M.

Todd Ames had apparently gone to the john because twenty minutes after entering his cabin Tobin had neither heard from nor seen the man.

Which caused a certain degree of resentment in Tobin. Standing up in a corner of the dark closet was not fun. At least it was big and mostly empty but still it was dull, particularly given the fact that Tobin had abandoned the chance to have some sort of tryst with Susan Richards to be here.

All he could do now, unfortunately, was wait. The large dusty closet was lit only by corridor light spilling into the louvered door.

Ten minutes later he had to risk going to the bathroom. He just couldn't hold it anymore.

He ran in and did the deed and ran back.

He'd just gotten the closet door closed when he heard footsteps coming down the corridor.

Tobin had made it easy for whoever might want to claim the personal effects of Iris Graves and Everett Sanderson.

He'd put everything right in the middle of the bed.

All the thief had to do was rummage through it, take what he or she wanted, and then Tobin would spring from the closet and trap the person.

It sure *sounded* simple enough . . .

The cabin doorknob rattled as it was turned first rightward and then leftward.

Tobin's heart began pounding so loudly he wondered if the intruder could hear it. Sweat started collecting under his arms and down his back and in his shoes. Flop sweat.

The door creaked open.

Either the intruder possessed burglary tools or knew how to use a credit card.

The door creaked shut.

A dark form stood in the center of the cabin, looking around, as if he suspected that he was indeed being spied upon.

No problem identifying the person. There'd been only one cowboy at the costume party tonight. Jere Farris.

The cowboy outfit had included a pair of spurs, which did not exactly lend themselves to stealth. As Farris crossed the room to the bed, thumbing on a flashlight whose beam was yellow and lurid in the gloom, his spurs began to jangle.

Farris set to work.

He went through the box belonging to Sanderson first. He picked up a variety of items, examined each, and then put them back.

Next he went through Iris Graves's material and it was here that he paused at great length, especially when he came to the notebook Tobin had so thoughtfully set out.

He thumbed through the pages to the middle section where she'd done most of her writing on the "Celebrity Circle" show. Then he said, "Sonofabitch."

Obviously Farris knew that Iris Graves had known something about the "Circle" crew.

The next set of footsteps were lighter than Farris's had been.

Both Tobin and Farris froze and stared at the cabin door, the knob of which was being shaken in a hopeless attempt to rattle it open.

Tobin watched Farris panic—whip his head around, his white Stetson nearly falling off, searching desperately for a place to hide.

Where else in a cabin like this *could* you hide?

The person at the cabin door now applied a credit card, just as Farris himself had done.

Farris stuffed the book inside his vest and started for the closet.

Wanting to see who else was coming to steal something from his cabin, Tobin obligingly opened the closet door and then put a finger to his lips and made a big *sssshing!* sound.

Farris, startled, almost yelled out something in surprise but Tobin gave him a double *sssh!* and that took care of him.

Tobin grabbed Farris by the wrist, yanked him inside, and then waited to see who came in next.

She had some kind of lantern, one of those bulky jobs you take camping to Montana. It looked all wrong with her Bo Peep getup. You would have thought that Cassie McDowell would have elected something more graceful and feminine.

Like Farris, she stood in the dark, orienting herself first. But it didn't take long for her to find the things piled on the bed. Tobin had put everything but a STEAL ME QUICK sign on the stuff.

Several times Farris in his goofy cowboy clothes leaned toward Tobin as if he wanted to whisper something but Tobin pointed a finger at him, implying that he'd punch Farris for making any sound at all.

Cassie went through the material in much the same order Farris had. Something seemed to interest her in Sanderson's belongings, though from the angle of the closet, Tobin could not see what. Then she began to work through Iris Graves's things.

Or started to, anyway.

She'd no more than lifted Iris's reporter's pad when somebody could be heard moving down the corridor.

Cassie stopped, killed the lantern.

In the shadows Tobin could hear all three of them breathing. They sounded as if they'd been running up and down stairs.

A hand wrenched the cabin doorknob.

"Oh, shit," Cassie said, though not loudly enough to be heard in the corridor.

Her eyes searched frantically about the cabin and came to rest, of course, on the louvered closet door.

Tobin opened it up, stuck out his head, grabbed her elbow, and jerked her in, clamping a hand over her mouth for good measure.

He got the closet door closed and then the three of them—Tobin, Cassie, and Farris (who'd moved down one, the way used-up guests did on the Carson show)—watched as Tarzan came into the room.

Kevin Anderson, macho guy that he was, had not brought a light along. Presumably this was because of his X-ray vision.

He went without pause to the bed and the material. He was, of course, neither as gentle nor as neat as Farris and Cassie had been. He made a quick mess of things, in fact, scattering items all over the bed. He reminded Tobin of a dog rooting for something buried.

The less he found that interested him, the more furious Anderson's search became.

Until the next set of footsteps came along.

Where Farris and Cassie had gotten scared, Anderson got angry.

He stood in the center of the cabin looking big and fit but vaguely silly in his fake leopard skin loincloth, making a large club from his fist.

Obviously he was simply going to deck whoever came through the door.

But, not wanting the next person to be scared off—he'd learned nothing so far but the person now trying the doorknob might just be the one—Tobin once again eased open the closet door and went, "Pssst!"

Anderson spun around as if somebody had struck him in the back of the head with a rock.

"Get in here!" Tobin whispered.

As the cabin door was starting to open, Anderson apparently got caught up in the moment and complied without any hassle.

Cassie moved down one inside the closet and Anderson took her place. Now there were Tobin, Anderson, Cassie, and Farris. Everything smelled cramped and sweaty. Only Cassie's perfume kept the closet from reeking like a locker room.

A beautiful hooker came in next. She'd brought one of those dinky pencil flashlights doctors use when they make you say "Ahhhh."

Tobin got a vicious elbow in the rib from Anderson. Cassie, who'd had more than her share to drink, had tottered into Anderson and so Tobin wound up getting the elbow. He wanted to curse and very loudly but he knew better. In here all he could say was, *"Ssshhh!"*

All of them leaned up to the louvers so they could watch as Susan Richards sorted through the debris Kevin Anderson had strewn all over the bed.

The problem was, Tobin realized, you couldn't see

whose stuff—Sanderson's or Iris's—she was going through because now it was all mixed up together.

Something caught her attention, though, because she leaned way over and started to examine it.

Tobin couldn't be sure if she picked it up and took it because about the time she would have been doing so, the cabin door opened up and there stood somebody else with a flashlight.

Todd Ames must have crept along the corridor on tiptoes because none of them had heard him at all.

Now Ames and Susan stood a few feet apart in the gloom, shining their lights on each other.

"Susan, what are you doing here?"

"I could ask the same question, Todd."

"I'm sick of this bullshit!" Anderson said and ripped open the closet door.

Susan screamed.

Ames threw on the lights and held up a .45 he'd concealed in his thick sueded Robin Hood belt.

Susan, seeing everybody come out of the closet, said, "What were you all doing in there?"

"Watching you," Tobin said. He nodded to Ames. "You'd better either use that or put it away."

Ames touched one side of his perfect gray hair and said, "Seems as if I should be the one giving the orders."

Anderson moved so quickly even Tobin was forced to admit he was impressed.

Anderson slapped Ames across the face and then simply took the gun from him.

Anderson said, "Now, Tobin, you little bastard, I want you to tell me what's going on here."

30

"So why don't we just get it over with?" Tobin said, once they'd all found various places to sit.

"Get what over with?" Cassie McDowell asked, reverting to TV. She was the naïve schoolteacher of "McKinley High, USA." Her Bo Peep garb had never seemed more appropriate.

"Gosh, I can't imagine," Tobin said. Then, "What the hell do you *think* I'm talking about? I told Jere and you that I had the personal effects of Iris Graves and Everett Sanderson in my room—and then each of you proceeded to break in. What the hell were you looking for?"

Kevin Anderson and Todd Ames had helped themselves to the quart of Wild Turkey Tobin had sitting on his bureau. They guzzled it without ice from transparent plastic glasses.

Ames said, "We don't have to answer a damn thing."

Susan Richards, lighting a cigarette, said, "I came here because I heard there was a party."

"Right," Tobin said, "so you jimmied the lock with a credit card and came in."

Tobin, as always when he was angry, paced. Being small and compact, he gave the impression of great energy as he did so. With his Burglar mask still on, he looked both greatly earnest and greatly comic.

He paused at Kevin Anderson and said, "I'm surprised you'd be afraid of him."

"Afraid of who?"

"Of Ken Norris."

Anderson's masculinity had been challenged. "Who said I was afraid of him?"

"If you hadn't been then you wouldn't have resorted to killing him."

Anderson set down his drink. He made his biceps bulky and his hands into fists. "You accuse me of killing him again, I'll punch your face in."

"Jesus, Kevin," Cassie said, "what we don't need is more violence."

Tobin turned to Jere Farris. "Why don't you share that notebook with us?"

"What notebook?" But he was flushing.

Tobin held out his hand.

Farris shook his head miserably—maybe he wouldn't have looked so miserable if he'd taken off his Stetson— and reached inside his leather vest. "Here."

Tobin tapped the notebook dramatically, the way a prosecuting attorney who'd trained at Warner Brothers would have.

"In this notebook," he said and thumped it again, rather enjoying himself now. "In this notebook is evidence that will convict one of you of Ken Norris's death—and the deaths of Iris Graves and Everett Sanderson."

"If you've got the evidence," said Todd Ames, smiling with capped teeth at Cassie, "then why don't you make a formal accusation?"

"Because as yet I haven't broken the code."

"Code?" Ames said.

"She wrote in her own shorthand. Not even her boss at *Snoop* can translate it."

He felt a genuine sense of relief pass through the five people packed into his tiny cabin.

He took to pacing again. He took to notebook-thumping again. He said, "You know what I think?"

Kevin Anderson said, "I don't know what you think but I also don't give a damn what you think."

"I think," said Tobin, undeterred, "that one of you killed him and that the rest of you are protecting that person." He thumped again. "But here's the trick. I also suspect that you're not sure which of you did it. You"—and he pointed to Cassie—"you may think it's Kevin and Kevin may think it's Todd and Todd may think—"

Todd Ames said, "You don't have a damn thing on any of us. You've got some queer notebook with some scrawlings in it, and that's all."

Jere Farris said, "And we've still got the show."

Tobin saw it then. Mention of the show made each of them smile. He saw how "Celebrity Circle" bound them up tight as blood. He said, "And that's why you're afraid that one of you is a killer. Because if that's the case, the show may well die. And your livelihoods will be all over." He turned to Farris. "What did you say about directing local TV news?"

Kevin Anderson threw back the last of the Wild Turkey and said, "I don't know about anybody else, but I'm leaving."

"Me too," Cassie said.

"One of you is a killer," Tobin said.

"You wave that goddamn notebook at us one more time," Anderson said, "and I'll put it someplace you won't like at all."

His anger served as a rallying point for the rest of them. Soon Tarzan was joined by a cowboy, a hooker, Robin Hood, and Florence Nightingale at the door.

"We're going back to the party," Jere Farris said, "and have a damn good time. You coming, Tobin?"

With that, they all laughed and left, slamming the door with undue finality.

The first thing Tobin did was go to the bathroom again.

Then he came out and lit up a cigarillo and took to pacing once more. His plan hadn't worked. He hadn't learned a damn thing.

Or so he thought until he began looking carefully at the jumble of personal effects on the bed.

Something was missing. He wasn't sure what. He just had the impression that not all the stuff Captain Hackett had given him was there now.

It took him ten minutes of sifting and ten minutes of trying to remember everything that Hackett had handed over before he realized what was gone.

Sanderson's newspaper clippings about the fire and the Indiana beauty contest. What bearing did they have on "Celebrity Circle"? And whose identity would they have exposed? Strange. Damn strange.

31

Friday: 12:53 A.M.

"Say, would you dance with me so my husband could take a picture of us?"

The woman, bigger than Tobin—which was not, after all, an especially impressive feat—had grabbed him just inside the restaurant where he'd gone in search of Cindy.

The woman was dressed as the Wicked Witch of the West and her husband as Teddy Roosevelt. The husband, drunk, tried aiming a Polaroid at Tobin. Everything here was, if anything, crazier than when Tobin had left. Two fat men did something like a polka with each other while their wives laughed so hard they pounded each other on the shoulder. The two fat men were up on a table. A waiter, in a snit, and probably a well-deserved snit, took a drunk's drink and poured it into a flower bowl, apparently telling the man he'd been cut off. The dance floor was darker now; only a feeble dawnlike hue of pink from a baby spotlight offered any illumination, and some of the scenes on the dance floor were reasonably pornographic, the frivolity of earlier hours having given way to pure—and understandable—lust.

"I've danced with everybody on 'Celebrity Circle,'" the woman said. "And Henry's taken my picture with every one. You're the last."

"Goody," Tobin said, letting her pull him onto the

floor and into his arms as the trio played "The Impossible Dream" as a samba.

"Smile," Henry said.

"I always liked you better than your partner on that review show," the woman said. "He was too snotty. He didn't like Robert Redford."

"Neither do I," Tobin said.

The woman, fiftyish, giggled. "Yes, but you're cute."

He supposed there was logic there somewhere.

As they danced, and Henry continued to punch out the Polaroids, Tobin glanced round the dance floor for sight of Cindy. But nothing. He saw all the others on the "Celebrity Circle" dais—and they all glowered at him whenever he made eye contact—except Cindy and Kevin Anderson.

My God, what if . . .

"It's such a great show," the Wicked Witch said.

"Beg pardon?"

"The show. 'Celebrity Circle.' It's great."

"Oh. Thanks. But I'm only doing this cruise and then I'm gone."

"Everybody looks like they're having so much fun." She giggled her annoying giggle again. The song was interminable. "I'd pay to be on that panel. I really would."

"Yes," Tobin said, on autopilot now, and only half-listening to her.

He was fearing the worst. That Kevin had sweet-talked Cindy . . .

The song, at last, ended and the woman said, rather threateningly really, "Did you get some good ones, Henry?"

"I got some wonderful ones, honey." He said

"shome" and he said "wunnerful" and saying so nearly fell over, from the booze, backwards.

"Thanks," Tobin said, extricating himself from her grasp. "I really enjoyed it."

And then he was off to the dais, pressing himself through dancers and sweet-talkers and boosters and sots, and at last he reached the dais and felt the laserlike collective glare of the "Celebrity Circle" group searing through him.

"Looks like Cindy dumped you again, Tobin," Jere Farris said.

"She wanted somebody who could get it up in less than a half-hour," said America's favorite school teacher, Cassie McDowell.

Only Susan Richards had the grace to look embarrassed at Cassie's drunken ugliness.

He turned back to the end of the table where Joanna Howard sat talking to a busboy who was obviously about her speed—neither one appeared to know how to put the moves on anybody.

He went up to her. "Have you seen Cindy?"

She glanced up and then frowned. "She . . . left."

Tobin cleared his throat. "Kevin?"

She paused. She tried to spare his feelings. "I really didn't see."

Which of course meant Yes.

The bastard had come back here after the confrontation in Tobin's cabin and taken Cindy away. But why, after the way he'd treated her last night, would she go?

Then he smiled to himself.

She'd go because women like Cindy seemed to derive perverse pleasure from men who treated them badly. Tobin had never understood this, and didn't care to, really.

When his gaze fell on Joanna again, he saw that she

was watching her lover, Jere Farris, in the arms of his wife on the dance floor.

Tobin said, "You can do better than him, Joanna. You really can."

She smiled with her soft forlorn eyes and said, "Weren't you the one asking about Cindy a few seconds ago?"

"Good point," he said, and went back to his cabin.

32

1:10 A.M.

Tobin, back in his cabin, calculated the time and decided to hell with it. He had to find out why somebody took the newspaper clippings relating to Everett Sanderson's presence on the cruise ship and left everything else.

He took one of Sanderson's brochures, looked at the phone number and town name and zip code rubber-stamped on the back of it, and then picked up the phone.

He first tried the number of the agency itself and got a ghostly answering machine, one of those recordings that sound as if they'd been made by a poltergeist. It said the agency was closed and would be open at 8:00 A.M. tomorrow, if tomorrow was a weekday. Then, fortunately, it left another number to call in case of emergency.

Tobin certainly considered this an emergency.

On the fourteenth ring a woman with a cigarette cough answered the phone.

Tobin said, "Hello?"

The woman kept coughing and finally said, "Who the hell is this anyway?"

The detective agency wasn't nearly as friendly as it had promised to be in the brochure.

33

It was while she was slathering her rather nice twenty-eight-year-old body with a bar of very soapy soap that Cindy thought she heard some kind of bump or thump in the cabin outside of Kevin Anderson's bathroom.

She stood very still, aware suddenly of just how naked naked really was, and held her breath the way she had when she'd been a little girl and played boogeyman with her brother and her brother was three steps away from finding her hiding under the bed—held her breath and strained her hearing so hard she got a slight headache.

But there was just the warm water beating on her body, beading on her body, and the pleasant exhaustion that came at the end of a long day.

Then she decided she was being paranoid. Maybe Kevin had just opened and shut a drawer with undue power. He liked doing stuff like that—flinging back doors and jerking up chairs from the floor and twisting them around to sit on. It was because he did things like that, or so she supposed, that she'd finally accepted his apologies for last night ("I've just been sort of uptight, babe," was the way he'd said it, not ever using the exact word sorry exactly but she knew that for a guy like him—he had, after all, had his own network series and there was the promise of another—that for a guy like him even those words had been difficult to say) and so, at the last, Tobin gone, she'd said, yes, all right, she'd go back to his cabin with him, both of them knowing of course what that meant.

Kevin had wanted to take her two steps inside the cabin door. The nun's outfit had really fired up most of the men. But inside its heavy black folds she'd run with sweat and insisted on taking a quick shower, during which time she'd started composing a letter to Aberdeen about how weird this trip was becoming, with a TV star practically begging her for her company.

A door slammed.

She couldn't be sure of it.

It might have been any number of other things— somebody drunk falling against the wall in the corridor, Kevin sliding back the closet door with his usual enthusiasm—but somehow she thought not.

Somehow she thought a door had slammed.

Tired of all her apprehension, she turned off the shower, slid back the door, and grabbed a big white fluffy towel.

She dried off quickly, took a smaller towel to use as a turban for her hair, and then left the slippery tiles and steamy air of the bathroom.

She found Kevin immediately and began screaming almost as immediately.

34 1:23 A.M.

"That little squirt on TV?" the woman said.

"That's me."

"What the hell you doin' callin' here at three in the morning?" Her voice had gotten much friendlier since he'd explained who he was. Fortunately, or so she confided, she'd always preferred him to Richard Dunphy.

"You know that a man named Everett Sanderson was murdered."

A mournful pause. Sigh. "Yep."

"He was your husband?"

"Nope. Brother-in-law. His wife died twenty years ago or so and he never remarried. Ever since he lived upstairs in our youngster's room. Him and Merle, that's my husband, they ran the agency together."

"That's what I'm calling about."

"The agency?"

"About what Everett was doing on the cruise."

Another pause. "You'd be wantin' to talk to Merle about that."

"Could you hand the phone over to him?"

"Can't."

"Asleep?"

"Gone."

"Where?"

Pause. "I really shouldn't be talkin' to you. Merle hates it when I talk to people about his business."

"When will he be back, Mrs. Sanderson?"

"Tomorrow morning sometime." Beat. "He's doin' a divorce case. One of those stakeout jobs. He'll be real tired. He'll want a big breakfast—three eggs and some sausages and some wheatcakes and some toast with peanut butter and jelly—then he'll want to roll right into bed."

"What would be a good time to call him?"

"Maybe two, three in the afternoon. Our time."

"All right." Then he thought of the newspaper clipping. "By the way, did your husband or Everett ever mention a man who died in a trailer fire named William Kelly?"

"How'd you find out about him?" She sounded suspicious.

"They have mentioned him then?"

"Of course they mentioned him. He was kin. A first cousin."

"What?"

"Sure. Hell, I was to his baptism. He was a good boy and then—"

"Then what?"

"Now I'm gettin' into agency business and that's where Merle can get mighty mad. You just call back like I told you to."

"But—"

"You just call back."

And then she hung up.

He had just decided to light up a cigarillo when a heavy hand fell many times on his cabin door.

He was up off the bed, frightened and puzzled, in seconds.

Captain Hackett stood in the door. You could tell he'd been drunk and had then gotten sober abruptly.

He looked old and he looked miserable. "It's happened again."

"What's happened?"

"A killing."

"Who?"

"Kevin Anderson."

"My God."

"Come on," the captain said, "and hurry."

35 2:01 A.M.

They had put him out in the corridor and they had put a white sheet over him and into the white sheet had soaked the red blood, his blood of course, that had come from the repeated shots in the chest.

He was tall enough that the sheet only reached to just below his knees. You got a good look at very hairy legs and soles with athlete's foot.

The costume party, which had still been going on even though the more sensible or more lustful had long since fled it, had brought out moth-to-flame onlookers. They stood now in their silly getups—Snow White and Teddy Roosevelt and Superman—watching as somber men in white jackets went in and out of the room. Occasionally Captain Hackett came out and asked them to please, please go back to the party and have a good time, that there had been another misfortune (he was a word man, was the captain) but there was nothing for them to fear. A few complained, a few more threatened, but they were too drunk and filled with the festivities to do anything but wobble back from where they'd come, along the deck of the cruise ship, the stars brilliant and timeless, the moon full and pagan. The band had never stopped playing and the air was filled with the playful, erotic strains of Cole Porter's "Love For Sale."

"You were taking a shower?"

"Tobin, please, don't I get a lawyer or something?"

Tobin went over and hunched down next to her. They were in Kevin Anderson's cabin. You could smell blood and other terrible things. You could see where, in falling over backwards from the force of the shots, Kevin Anderson had smashed a lamp and cracked a mirror. There was a sinister aspect to the room now. The lights seemed very bright. The carpet was splotchy red. Now Tobin sensed what detectives must feel when they come on a murder scene. There was something pornographic about it all.

Cindy was wrapped in a towel. She sat on a small footstool. She looked very young.

Captain Hackett said, "You haven't answered my question, young lady."

"Tobin?" she said, appealing to him.

"Why don't you just answer him, Cindy? He's not trying to trap you into anything—or if he is—I won't let him. He's just trying to find out what went on here."

She glanced up at the captain. "I don't want you to think I'm . . . well, easy, or anything."

"The other night while you were taking a shower, a man died. Tonight you're taking another shower and another man dies. I'd like to know why."

"I don't know why."

"You didn't hear anything?"

"Some kind of . . . crash or something, I guess."

"Crash?"

"Something fell over."

"But you didn't come out to see what it was?"

"I was in the shower."

"Did you call out?"

"Call out?"

"For Anderson? Did you call out to see if he was all right?"

"I guess not, no."

"Why not?"

"I . . . don't know why not."

And then she broke down, sobbing.

Tobin slid his arm around her and said, "You don't really think she had anything to do with this, do you?"

Hackett said, "No, I suppose not."

"Then can't we leave everything else till morning?"

Hackett glanced at the door through which came a red-faced Dr. Devane. He'd obviously been awakened from a boozy slumber. He wore a bathrobe and slippers that flapped and he carried a little black bag. "Evening," he said.

"I'd like to get Cindy out of here," Tobin said. "Any reason I can't?"

"I guess not," Hackett said.

Cindy, still sobbing, rose and clutched the towel tightly to herself. When she got very close to the captain she said, "I don't want you to get the wrong idea about me."

"Oh, no," the captain said. "I'd never do that."

As Tobin took Cindy's arm and helped her through the door, he saw Hackett shake his head and frown. Obviously he felt it was a bit late for Cindy to start defending her virtue.

36

2:45 A.M.

"I'll make love if you want to."

"Boy, you really sound enthusiastic," Tobin said.

"Maybe it would help me."

They were in his cabin in the darkness and in his bed.

"Medicinal purposes, eh?" Tobin said.

"You don't have to be sarcastic."

"Maybe it isn't such a good idea."

"Don't you like me anymore?"

"It isn't that."

"Then what is it?"

"It's just all so goddamned confusing. The killings, and you not sleeping with me because you respect me too much, and why the 'Celebrity' people won't help Captain Hackett find out what's going on."

She nuzzled him and he responded but something kept him back.

"Maybe we'd both feel better," she said.

"I thought you respected me so much."

"I just feel so lost and so lonely. I wish I were back in Kansas City and Aberdeen and I were going shopping."

"All right," he said. "I'll do it."

She sort of thumped him. "Gee, you sound like you're doing me some kind of favor or something. Nobody's ever sounded like that with me before."

Tobin said, "We're both doing each other a favor. That's how you've got to look at it."

Just before they went to sleep, half an hour later, Cindy said, "You know, two weeks ago I would have paid money to just hang around real celebrities. But now I don't know."

Tobin sort of muttered a response. Then he heard the echoes of what she said and he thought of what the woman he'd danced with earlier that night—the Wicked Witch of the West—had said about paying money just to be a part of "Celebrity Circle."

Tobin said, "I've got it."

"What?"

"'Payday.'"

"What?"

"'Payday.' I think I figured it out."

"Well, I'm real happy for you."

"What're you so mad about?"

"We get done and you roll over and you don't say anything."

"Like what?"

"Like how much you enjoyed it?"

"I did enjoy it. Did you?"

Apparently she was in a mood to pay him back. All she said was, "Sort of, I guess."

Then she turned over and in two minutes was snoring softly.

Or maybe was faking snoring softly. With Cindy you couldn't be sure.

But all Tobin could really concentrate on anyway was "payday."

In the morning he planned to confront one of the remaining celebrities with what he'd figured out.

The $10,000 *Snoop* was going to pay him glowed a vivid green in his dreams.

37

9:01 A.M.

Alicia Farris answered the door. She wore a sheer pink robe and dark glasses and smoked a very long cigarette.

"I take it you're not room service," she said to Tobin. He wore a white shirt and blue blazer and gray slacks and black socks and cordovan loafers. He smoked a cigarillo.

"I'd like to talk to you and Jere."

"Who the hell is it?" Jere said from the deep interior shadows.

"You can see what pleasant company he is in the morning. Why don't you stop back?"

"Why don't you close the door and get some clothes on him and then let me in?"

"What's going on?"

"I've figured it out."

"Figured what out?"

"Why all these people are getting killed."

"You're turning asshole on us, aren't you, Tobin?"

"I'm getting to the truth."

"How noble."

"Tell him to screw off," Jere Farris shouted from the bed.

"I'll be waiting," Tobin said, "and I don't want to wait any longer than two minutes."

She slammed the door.

Tobin walked down to the edge of the deck and

leaned on the rail and looked at the green water and the blue sky and the white gulls. In the distance there were other boats. Tonight they would be docking. Everything needed to be concluded by then.

He was lost to his thoughts when he heard somebody say, "Don't you hate morning light? It has no pity."

He turned and saw Susan Richards next to him. She wore a festive red scarf over her black hair and a white pleated blouse and tight black slacks. With her red mouth and shades she looked very Hollywood. She was a pleasure to look at.

All this was ruined by the fact that she was drunk. He knew it by the smell of booze on her and by the way she weaved when she spoke. Hadn't she gone to bed? Had she spent the whole night drinking? She must have tried to sober up by showering and putting on fresh clothes. It hadn't worked.

She said, "But then so few things do these days."

"Hmmm?"

"Pity. There's so little of it these days."

"Oh."

"You're aware I'm drunk."

"Yes."

"Perhaps I have a problem in that area. I've been told by three husbands and four shrinks that that may well be the case."

"I'm sorry."

"I like you, Tobin. Have I told you that?"

"No. But I certainly accept it as a compliment. And I like you."

"Wouldn't it be ducky if we could do something about it?" She paused, tossed her head as if it were something she wanted to be rid of. "I don't mean just go to bed. I mean . . . have a relationship or something."

"That would be very 'ducky.'"

"I used that word because you use it in your column sometimes."

"It's when I'm trying to be British, I suppose. I'm not sure it ever comes off."

She laughed. She sounded miserable. "We're a lot alike."

"How's that?"

"No confidence in ourselves. You're always putting yourself down, and I'm always fearing the worst."

This time when she started to stumble backwards, he had to catch her by the wrist. It was a slender wrist, a lovely wrist.

He said, "Would you do me a favor?"

"What's that?"

"Would you go back to your cabin and lie down?"

"I came here to tell you something."

"Just sleep for a few hours and then maybe we'll have lunch together."

She slid her glasses down to the tip of her nose. "Do you have some pressing business or something?"

"Yes," he said. "Yes, I do."

"No wonder I'm so insecure. I practically ask you to marry me and you tell me to lie down. Alone."

He leaned in and kissed her on the cheek. She was weaving and wobbling again. He waved to a white-jacketed steward.

"Would you walk with Miss Richards to her cabin?" Tobin said, pressing a five-dollar bill into the steward's hand.

"I really need to talk to you," Susan said but by then the steward had taken her arm. He seemed very good and very practiced at this sort of thing. Within moments they had disappeared around the curve of the deck.

Tobin went back to the Farrises' cabin.

38 9:14 A.M.

"He wasn't blackmailing you, was he?"

"I don't have to answer any of your stupid god-damned questions," Jere Farris said.

"He wasn't blackmailing you—but you were paying him to be on the show. Probably a certain percentage."

Alicia Farris had opened the cabin curtains. The sunlight was rich and yellow and you could see clearly the red nub in the carpeting and where there was a stain of some sort on the sheet and the last wisp of steam on the bathroom mirror from the shower being run hot and long.

Jere wore a blue button-down shirt and jeans. His blue eyes needed some Visine. He wore no shoes or socks. He had a fierce red bunion on the big toe of his left foot. He smoked one of his wife's long white cigarettes. In the yellow sunlight the smoke was silver blue. He said, "I'm getting sick of you, Tobin. In case I haven't told you that already, I mean."

"That's what 'payday' meant. Every time you got a check, you had to pay him part of it."

"That's bullshit," Farris said.

Alicia, sitting on the edge of the bed near where the sheet was stained, said quietly, "Why don't we just tell him, Jere?"

"Why don't you just keep out of it, bitch?"

She leaned over and with a great deal of expertise slapped him once very hard across the mouth. You could see tears in his eyes and a pinpoint of blood on his lower lip. "I'll put up with your stupid little girlfriends, Jere, but I won't put up with anything else."

Tobin pulled his eyes away. He did not want to be in this room at this moment. There was a slow and sad and long-standing anger here—an anger about to become rage—one of the worst kind, one borne of humiliation and debasement. There was nothing uglier to see. Nothing.

Alicia turned to Tobin and said, "It was very simple. He had all the power, Ken Norris did. He could go to the syndication company and get any one of us fired at any time. He knew it and we knew it. So we had to pay him ten percent of our salaries to stay on the show." She exhaled silver blue smoke of her own. "Face it, Tobin, without that show none of us would have any career at all. It was worth the ten percent."

Tobin said, "Iris Graves knew that. That had to be the story she was working on. And Sanderson the private detective knew that too. I can understand why one of you would kill them and Ken Norris. But why Kevin Anderson?"

"Because he was sick of the sham," Farris said, slamming his fist on the table. "He was going to talk to the press as soon as he got back."

"So everybody in your group knew this?"

Alicia nodded.

"And apparently," Tobin said, "added Kevin to the list."

"I didn't kill anybody, if that's what you're thinking." His petulance was getting irritating again.

"I think," Alicia said with a kind of defiant dignity, "that Tobin suspects it's me." She smiled at her husband. It was a pleasant smile to see. "After all, dear, I'm the only one with any balls in the family."

"She didn't kill anybody, either," Farris said.

"One of your group did," Tobin said, "in order to prevent the story from coming out."

"It would have made us laughingstocks," Alicia said, her voice quiet again. "It's bad enough to be has-beens but to have to pay kickbacks on TV—you can imagine what the press would have done to us."

Tobin was about to speak when a noise, almost vulgar on the fresh ocean air and on such a sunny day and on such blue water, violated the peace of the cruise ship.

There was no mistaking what it was, the noise.

It was the sound of a gun being fired.

"My God," Alicia said.

But Tobin was already out the door.

39

9:26 A.M.

Six doors away, Todd Ames, looking as if he were preparing for a *GQ* photo shoot—white button-down shirt, apricot colored ascot, white linen pants, steel gray hair in perfect shape—leaned to the side of Susan Richards's door. He appeared to be in clinical shock.

As Tobin reached him, he saw that .45 dangled from Ames's left hand. Tobin recognized the weapon as Ames's own. Ames did not seem aware that he held the gun.

Tobin glanced at him, then pushed inside.

The curtains were still drawn. The room stank of bourbon. The bed was a mess. There was the scent of sleep and sweat and vomit. With the door closed, Tobin felt as if he had stepped down into a deep hole that had sealed itself behind him.

She sat curled in a chair. She was naked. There was for the moment nothing erotic about her. Indeed her nakedness was terrifying because it was obviously symbolic of her mental state.

She turned her beautiful aging face to look up at Tobin. She said, "You know the funny thing?"

"No," he said, "no, I don't know the funny thing."

"Prison isn't what scares me."

"What scares you, Susan?"

"The photographers."

"Why do they scare you?"

185

He wished it were light in here. He wished it did not smell so womb-warm. He wished her eyes did not look so unfocused.

"The way they used to follow Marilyn Monroe around. You remember?"

"Yes."

"They'd get right up to her and she'd start to cry and you could see the panic in her eyes. That's what scares me."

"You killed them, then?"

"Yes."

"Why?"

She laughed. "Tobin, it was the only career I had. Once it came out that I'd had to pay to be on it—"

"God," he said, and sank down onto the ottoman. He leaned back a bit toward the bureau where he could smell the sweet perfume and even sweeter sachet. He liked the female smells and for the first time he became aware of the sexuality of her naked body. He felt ashamed that lust had as always triumphed over compassion.

"What was the gunshot? You trying to kill yourself?"

She laughed and for a moment sounded genuinely delighted. "What, and ruin my makeup? No, I was just trying to get attention, Tobin." She pointed with an elegant hand to a hole in the wall. "I just fired the gun because I thought it would sound good. I had to do something." Then her face grew sad again, like a small girl hearing terrible news, and she said, "You didn't want me to be the killer, did you?"

"No."

"That's very nice of you."

He raised his head again and stared at her. "When the captain comes, don't say anything."

"What?"

"Don't say anything until you've got a lawyer."

"It doesn't matter, Tobin. It really doesn't."

"It matters to me."

"I appreciate that."

Tobin said, "Why kill Sanderson too? Iris Graves had discovered what was going on—Ken Norris demanding a part of your salary—but why Sanderson?"

"Because he was helping the reporter and even if he hadn't wanted to, he would have exposed me."

"They worked together?"

"Yes."

He was about to ask her more but the door creaked open and Captain Hackett put his head inside.

"I just had a conversation with Todd Ames, Miss Richards," Captain Hackett said. "He told me what you tried to do and what you confessed to. Are those things true?"

"Remember what I said about a lawyer," Tobin said.

"Yes, Captain," Susan Richards said. "They are true."

"God," Tobin said. "God."

She'd been right, Susan had. He would not have been unhappy to learn that the killer was Jere Farris or Todd Ames or Cassie McDowell or even Alicia Farris. But he genuinely liked Susan Richards. Genuinely.

Captain Hackett said, "I'll be outside, Tobin. You help her get dressed and then bring her out. All right?"

Tobin did the only thing he could do. He nodded.

40 11:14 A.M.

"Forget the part where you think she's crazy."

"Forget it? Why?"

"Because if she's crazy, then people feel sorry for her and if they feel sorry for her, then it's just another story about some pathetic has-been TV star. But if she willfully and coldly set out to do in all these people—ape shit is the word I'm looking for here, Tobin."

"That's two words."

"Whatever. Ape shit is what our readers will do. AGING PRIME TIME QUEEN KILLS TO KEEP HER SHAME SECRET. It needs some work but it's a good peg. You earned your dough, pally."

"Thanks."

"Hey, you get seven grand and you sound miserable."

"I am miserable. I happened to like Susan. And what's this seven grand stuff?"

"Expenses."

"What expenses?"

"I told you already. Phone calls and stuff."

"What's 'stuff?'"

"Jesus, all right. We should be celebrating and we're haggling. Seventy-five hundred then."

"First you said ten, then you said eight, and now you're saying seventy-five hundred."

"Just get some good pictures, OK?"

The editor of *Snoop*, who probably not only watched "Celebrity Handyman" but liked it, hung up.

Tobin went into one of the ship's eight bars.

41

There was a kind of ritual involved in getting drunk to forget. First of all, you wanted to reach the first level of drunkenness very quickly so you drank drinks with gin in them. In this case, Tobin used martinis. Then you wanted to sit by yourself with a window to stare through, which was easy enough to do on a cruise ship. Then you wanted to be left entirely alone with only a jukebox for company. This tiny dark bar, festooned with nautical symbols, had a jukebox that ran to Sinatra and Nat King Cole and Johnny Mathis. You couldn't ask for more than that.

It didn't always work as you intended it to, of course.

There was a certain kind of drunkenness that was just bloody wonderful, when you reached the exact point where sadness and despair meshed—there was an almost overwhelming and perverse sweetness to it.

Unfortunately, Tobin must have gone right past it without noticing it because, almost as if he'd been in a car accident, he looked up and saw a gigantic bartender in white shirt and white ducks and white apron leaning in and hauling him out of the booth.

"You've had enough for this afternoon, Mr. Tobin," the bartender said.

Enough? How long had he been drinking. Enough?

190   ≈

He couldn't possibly have had more than fourteen or fifteen martinis. So what if he did kind of trip and fall on his last journey to the jukebox ("Strangers in the Night" just kept sounding better and better). He tripped; was that a capital offense or what?

"Come on now, Mr. Tobin. Come on now."

42

You wake up and you can't remember anything. Nothing at all. You need to pee and you're afraid you need to barf and then you're afraid because you can't remember anything.

He reconstructed, or tried to: Susan Richards had attempted suicide but had failed and had then confessed to Todd Ames that she'd killed the four people. Then Tobin, sad because it was Susan, had gone to get drunk. "Scoobey-doobey-doo" kept playing in his head. That and Kent cigarettes. He definitely (well, sort of definitely) recalled buying a package of Kent cigarettes and smoking them. One by one till they were all gone.

He lay there then and pressed the remote control on his nightstand. He might as well be viewing while he was preparing himself for the enormous task of emptying his bladder and taking a shower.

No easy thing to move your leg and put your foot on the floor and then get up and go into the bathroom.

And then for no reason he thought of his daughter (the way fragments of memory assault you during a hangover) and how her hair had looked so red in the sunlight at her cap-and-gown graduation and how he'd hugged her and . . .

The movie was *Death Wish 9* in which Charles Bronson, now an octogenarian, is dedicated to keeping safe the lives of his fellow prisoners in an old folks' home.

They'd managed to get sex into the film by having the extremely sexy day nurse wear a see-through uniform.

Finally, he couldn't take it any longer—not the movie, his bladder.

He forced his leg off the bed and then his other leg and then he went and had himself a shower.

When he came out he opened a beer left over from last night's frolic and was just having his first sip when the phone rang.

It was an operator and she wanted to know if he was the Mr. Tobin who had called the residence of a Mr. Sanderson and Tobin said he was and then she said go ahead please.

"Mr. Tobin, this is Everett Sanderson's brother. You were supposed to call me this afternoon." He sounded angry.

"Damn, I completely forgot. I'm sorry."

"You called last night and was asking the missus some questions about my cousin who died in that trailer fire."

"Yes, I was, Mr. Sanderson."

"I'd like to know why."

"I wanted to know why your brother was on the cruise ship."

"Did they find out who killed him yet?"

"Yes."

There was a long pause. Then a noise that might have been a sob. "There ain't nothin' bad enough that can happen to that man."

"It's a she."

"A woman?"

"Yes."

"Bullshit. No woman could kill Everett."

Given the circumstances, Tobin decided to overlook the ridiculous remark.

"What the hell did she have to do with Everett?"

"He knew about Ken Norris skimming the money from the 'Celebrity Circle' cast. She didn't want that known."

"I don't know what you're talkin' about."

"Your brother was working with a woman named Iris Graves from a newsstand paper called *Snoop*."

"*Snoop*. Everett read it all the time but he sure as hell didn't work for it."

"You're sure?"

"My brother went on that boat to talk to Mandy Nichols."

"Who?"

"Mandy Nichols. She was married to a cousin of ours." Then he mentioned the name of the man in the newspaper clipping—the one who'd been burned to death in the trailer fire.

Tobin leaned back against the headboard. "Why would he be trailing Mandy Nichols here?"

"Because she killed our cousin—and damn near killed their little girl right along with him."

Tobin explained about the newspaper clipping he'd discovered along with Everett's personal effects. "Why didn't it mention a little girl?"

"They didn't find her till next day. She'd crawled away from the fire, then collapsed out in the woods. They'd assumed at first that Mandy had taken her along." He cursed. "'Course Mandy with her fancy notions didn't plan to take nobody along. My cousin was the kind of man who woulda tracked her down and she knew it. So she tried to kill both of 'em—her husband and her daughter."

"And Everett's been tracking her all these years?"

"Yes. Till about a year ago when we found her."

"Mandy?"

"Right."

"Where was she?"

"Hollywood. That was always her thing. To live in Hollywood. Couldn't sing, couldn't dance, couldn't really even act much based on what I saw in her high school plays. But she did have a good face and a good body. I gotta give her that."

"So Everett confronted her?"

"He tried. She had him arrested several times. He tried to tell the police what had happened—how she'd hooked up with these so-called actors who were down here on location and the three of them helped her douse the trailer with gasoline and then set it up."

"You're sure it was the actors?"

"Positive. It had rained three or four hours after the fire and the sheriff found four sets of tracks in the morning—three male ones and then Mandy's."

"So Everett tracked Mandy down after all these years."

"He sure did. We run this small investigation agency but every chance he'd get to work on the case, he'd take it. He'd keep going to the sheriff but he said we needed more evidence—then they started saying the case was so old they couldn't do anything about it even if they'd wanted to."

"So why did he board this cruise?"

"Because something new had come up."

"What was that, Mr. Sanderson?"

There was a pause, and then Sanderson told him. And then Tobin had to move very, very quickly.

43

7:41 P.M.

"I need to see Susan Richards," Tobin said, pushing through Captain Hackett's door without knocking.

The captain, dining alone at his desk, looked up abruptly and said, "What the hell's wrong with you?"

"I said I need to see Susan Richards."

"Why?"

"I want you to call the steward who's standing guard and tell him I'm going to be there in fifteen minutes and that I'm being permitted to go in and talk to her. But first I need a key to her cabin."

"I put her in the cabin two doors down from where she was staying—for safekeeping. Care to tell me what the hell's going on?"

Tobin said, "I don't think she's our killer."

The captain put down his fork. "Do you know what the hell you're talking about?"

Tobin shook his head. "I'm afraid I do, Captain. I'm afraid I do."

44

Susan Richards's room smelled of gentle perfume and cigarette smoke. The blinds were drawn, the bed properly made, all her cosmetics neatly arranged on the bureau.

Tobin started first in the bureau drawers. He found nothing except the expected lingerie, blouses, scarves.

He closed the final drawer and moved on to the closet. He paused once and clipped off the light because he heard somebody coming down the corridor. The footsteps were loud, squeaky with leather.

Then they moved on past.

Tobin resumed his search, finding two leather suitcases set side-by-side in the back of the closet.

He turned on the light again and hauled both suitcases to the bed.

The first suitcase was stuffed with more cosmetics. Running to wrinkle cream, and moisturizer, and Scandinavian elixirs that promised all sorts of miracles, they were sad reminders of how uncomfortably many beautiful women deal with impending age.

In the second suitcase he found the two things of note: the small black and white photograph he'd seen Susan Richards holding the other day by the swimming pool and a folded letter identical to the one that Cindy McBain had seen stuffed under Kevin

≈ *197*

Anderson's door—the one with the Xerox of the infant. The one all the "Celebrity Circle" panelists had received.

Tobin compared the small photograph to the Xerox image on the paper. They were identical.

He knew now that everything Everett Sanderson's brother had told him on the phone was true.

He picked up the phone, dialed the Farris cabin.

Alicia Farris answered, "Hello."

"Hello, Alicia. This is Tobin."

"Oh. Hello." She did not sound the least happy to hear from him. After this afternoon he was hardly surprised.

"I need to speak to Jere."

"He's resting."

"It's important."

There was a pause. "Susan Richards is being charged with these murders. The scandal will destroy the show. What the hell more do you want, Tobin?"

"I want to speak to Jere."

"You sonofabitch."

But she did not hang up. In the background she could be heard telling her husband who was on the phone. Jere cursed. Bedsprings squeaked. He said, "What the hell do you want?"

"I need you to answer a question for me very carefully."

"Why should I?"

Tobin sighed. "It's important, Jere. That's why."

Ice rattled in a glass, which helped explain why Jere sounded half-bagged. "What's your question?"

"The night before last, did Joanna Howard push a love letter to you under your door?"

"Why the hell would that be any business of yours?"

"Answer me. Please."

"No."

"That's all I wanted to know."

As he was hanging up, he heard Jere sputtering another angry response.

45

"You always look so bundled up," Cindy said. "Slacks and long-sleeve blouses. You should let yourself go, especially on a cruise like this. You've got a nice shape."

They were in Joanna Howard's cabin and drinking wine. White wine and lots of it. Too much of it, in fact. Cindy felt positively drunk.

Late this afternoon she'd run into Joanna in one of the lounges. They'd had a steak sandwich together and then they'd come back to Joanna's to relax. Joanna reminded Cindy a bit of Aberdeen. She was full of questions about Cindy's life. The men she'd known and the places she'd gone and the best dresses she'd ever owned—but mostly about the men she'd known. Cindy felt like a movie star being interviewed by a slightly agog reporter—just the way Aberdeen always made her feel. But Cindy knew what Joanna was doing. She was trying to get over a broken heart because just this afternoon Jere Farris had informed her that he was breaking off their relationship.

Cindy sneezed.

"Catching cold?"

"Allergies. They just come up."

"Need a Kleenex?"

Cindy rooted about in her purse. "I've got one here." She waved it like a tiny white flag of surrender, then applied it to her nose. She filled it in a single blow.

"I'm sorry about Jere," Cindy said.

She sat on the couch with her feet on the coffee table. Joanna sat across the room, scrunched up in an easy chair.

"It's just as well," Joanna said.

The funny thing, Cindy thought, was that even though Joanna was throwing back the wine, she didn't sound drunk at all.

"It sure is," Cindy said, trying to sound brave on Joanna's behalf. "You'll find somebody twice as nice. Twice as nice."

Joanna touched her stomach. "Need to go to the bathroom. You want some more wine?"

"I can get it, hon. You just take care of your bladder."

Joanna grinned. She had a perfectly wonderful grin. "You're so nice."

"So are you."

On the way to the bathroom, Joanna passed by Cindy and touched her on one of her big toes. "You're a good friend of mine."

"Well, considering that you work with TV stars all day and I'm just a secretary, I consider that a compliment."

"An executive secretary."

"Well, yes, I guess that's true. An executive secretary."

"Be right back."

As soon as the bathroom door closed, Cindy sneezed this huge sneeze and then found herself with a wet nose and no Kleenex.

On unsteady feet, she got up and began looking for a box of tissues.

She opened the first bureau drawer she came to and

while she did find a box of Kleenex Boutique, she also found something else.

She was staring at the something else when she heard the bathroom door open up.

"Cindy. What the hell are you doing in my bureau?" Joanna said. She didn't sound cordial anymore. Not at all.

"I was just looking for Kleenex and I found . . ." And then her eyes dropped to the small black and white photograph.

She had seen a copy of this in the envelope slid under the door in Kevin Anderson's cabin and—

"My God," Cindy said. "You're the one who . . ."

But she didn't have time to finish the rest of the sentence because Joanna had magically produced a gun.

Cindy stared at it in disbelief.

She was a secretary from Kansas City (well, all right, an *executive* secretary) and guns just weren't a part of her life.

Not at all . . .

46

"She's your daughter, isn't she?"

"I don't know what you're talking about."

"What did they do to make her want to kill them?"

"Who?"

"You know who. Ken Norris and Kevin Anderson."

"I thought we were friends, Tobin."

"We are friends, Susan. I'm trying to stop anybody else from being killed." He paused. "She's your daughter, isn't she, Joanna Howard?"

"No."

"You're lying."

"As I said, I don't know what you're talking about."

"You thought she died in the trailer with your husband but she didn't. I talked to Everett Sanderson's brother—she crawled away from the blaze and the police found her in the morning."

"I'd like a cigarette."

"I don't have any."

"Why don't you ask the steward outside the door?"

"In a minute."

Susan sighed and let her head drop. Even in a loose gray workshirt and wrinkled jeans—and utterly without makeup—she was still beautiful. Fading as she approached her mid-forties but beautiful nonetheless.

They were in the cabin where Susan was being held. Sometimes people passed by in the corridor. Some of them whistled and some of them laughed. It seemed to

Tobin that at this moment no one on the entire planet had any right to whistle let alone laugh.

He stood three feet away from her. There was no doubt at all that he was her inquisitor. He wished it did not have to be this way but there was no choice. Not any longer.

He said, "You did a good job when you ran away from the trailer, Susan. Just enough plastic surgery that nobody back home would recognize you. Not right off, anyway. But you didn't count on the Sanderson brothers and you didn't count on your own daughter."

Susan looked up finally. Her face was ruined in the way a stroke victim's face is sometimes ruined. A look carved into the face forever. She said, "She's crazy, you know." She was starting to choke and cry.

"They helped you, didn't they—Ken Norris and Kevin Anderson—they helped you burn down the trailer, didn't they?"

She nodded, continued crying.

"They came to a small town to make a movie and you were dazzled—only your young husband was a very jealous man and wouldn't let you go when they made you promises about Hollywood—and so the only way out you could see was to burn down the trailer. Along with your husband and your daughter—and start all over again as Susan Richards."

He got up and she came at him and he could see now she was just as crazy as she'd accused her daughter of being.

He slapped her across the mouth once, with something like expertise, and pushed her on the bed.

He stood over her and said, "That's how you got your start in Hollywood, wasn't it? You were sleeping with them and they helped you burn down the trailer and so you were all locked in together. They had to help you succeed. Did they know your daughter was in the trailer that night?"

"No," she said softly. "I told them she and her father were out of town. They just thought they were helping me get a new start—burning down the trailer and sneaking out in the middle of the night. I was . . . crazy. All I could think of was getting rid of my daughter and husband and—" She rolled over on her stomach and put her head down and the sobs were so hard that the entire bed bounced.

He wanted to go over and slide his arm around her—he could not imagine how you could hold in your mind the fact that you had tried to kill your own child—and offer her whatever mixture of hatred and pity he felt for her.

But instead he said, "Jere Farris was a part of this, too, wasn't he? The other night Joanna tried to tell me she'd slipped a love letter under his door—but it was a Xerox of her baby picture, the one she left with Norris and Anderson before she killed them. She killed Sanderson and Iris Graves because they'd figured out who she was too. She didn't have any choice."

There was a knock.

Tobin kept his eyes on her as he went to get the door. When he opened it, the room was filled with the scent of the ocean. The steward stood there. "The captain asked me to check with you after ten minutes. To see if everything was all right." The steward carried a formidable walkie-talkie.

"Tell him everything's fine."

The steward nodded and closed the door.

When Tobin turned back, she was gone. He went over and sat in the easy chair and listened to her pee in the toilet.

When she came out she said, "Can you imagine her

life, Tobin? Can you imagine how I've destroyed it? Her own mother trying to kill her."

"I know." Suddenly he was tired of her self-pity. It was her daughter who should be pitied.

"I want you to tell her that I don't expect her to forgive me. But that I do ask her to understand that I was very young and that her father was very cruel."

"She was your daughter."

"Just tell her that, Tobin. Just tell her that."

He got up and put his hands in his pockets and began to pace.

He turned abruptly for the door.

"Where are you going, Tobin?" she said.

"Where the hell else?" he said. "To find your daughter."

47

8:51 P.M.

"Where's Jere?"

"Went for a walk," Alicia Farris said at her cabin door. "What the hell do you want with him?" She was drunk.

He ran the length of the deck and found no sight of Jere Farris. He found a phone in a lounge and called the captain. He explained as concisely as he could who Joanna Howard really was. "Find her before she kills Farris," he said.

He was back on the deck, headed for Cindy's cabin when he sensed rather than saw someone step from the shadows behind him. He'd been aware of a presence ever since leaving the lounge a few minutes ago.

She put the gun into his ribs, jamming it hard, and said, "I want you to help me get in to see my mother."

"I can't do that. She's under guard."

"I overheard your conversation with the captain. All you need to do is give the word."

"They're looking for you."

"I just want you to get me inside her room."

He saw her face finally, there in the moonlight. For the first time he saw a resemblance between the two women. Surgery had altered Susan Richards's face. What they shared was their insanity.

She prodded him with the gun.

The steward glanced up. "You going in again?"

"Yes."

He started to say something as he stood there in front of the door, officious in his whites, his walkie-talkie impressive, but Joanna spoiled all that by catching him a hard clean blow with the butt of her gun on the side of his head.

He went down in a heap.

She grabbed the doorknob and pushed the door inward. Then she said, "Get him in here so nobody sees him."

Tobin dragged the man inside.

"Tie him up and gag him," Joanna said, once the door was locked behind them.

Then she turned and looked at the woman on the bed. Tobin saw for the first time pieces of blood and flesh on Joanna's long-sleeved white blouse. Jere Farris's blood and flesh. She had gotten them all now. All except the one who mattered most.

Susan Richards was barely conscious. Next to her on the bed was a prescription bottle of sleeping pills. This time her suicide attempt had been for real. He said, panicked, "She's dying."

"From what?"

Tobin was still trying to adjust to the contrast between the shy, self-spoken Joanna and this harsh, singular young woman. "Sleeping pills and alcohol."

In two steps Joanna was at her mother's bedside. She leaned over and pulled the semiconscious woman up by the collar of her blouse.

"You killed my father, you bitch!" Joanna cried, and then began shaking her in a frenzy. "You killed my father, do you understand?"

She pushed her back down on the bed.

"I want a drink, Tobin."

There was the fifth of scotch from which Susan Richards had been drinking. Tobin went over and got them both drinks.

She took hers and said, "Sit in that chair over there where I can see you."

"What are you going to do?"

"We, Tobin, you and I. We're going to sit here and watch her die."

"I can't let you do it, Joanna."

She waved the gun at him. "You can stop me?"

He sighed and went over and sat in the armchair facing hers.

On the bed Susan Richards moaned and babbled. She sounded as if she were coming out of deep anesthesia.

People passed by talking. There were parties going on all over the boat. Tobin and Joanna sat in their chairs and watched a woman die.

"For what it's worth, Ken Norris and the others didn't know you were in that trailer that night," Tobin said.

"Don't talk."

He watched her then. She just stared at the woman on the bed. Her face, pretty if plain, was without expression. The .45 in her lap looked ludicrous until you noticed what he assumed was Jere Farris's blood.

Susan Richards began convulsing a few minutes later.

Tobin started to get up. Joanna leveled the gun at him, waved him back down.

They sat and watched some more.

At one point Susan wet her pants. Then she began crying. She wasn't conscious at all now.

Joanna continued to stare at her mother. Just stare. "Go check her pulse," she said finally.

"Why don't you let me call the doctor?" Tobin said. "Maybe there's still time."

"Check her pulse."

Tobin leaned over Susan. Her skin was cold and sweaty. He checked for a pulse in her wrist and then in her neck and then in her ankle. It was very faint.

He turned back to Joanna. He said, "She's dead."

"You're lying."

"Check for yourself."

"She just made a sound a minute ago."

"Apparently it was her last sound."

"You're like all the others. A liar."

He stood aside from the bed, inviting her to check for herself.

"Goddammit," Joanna said as she got up. "I wanted there to be pain. I wanted her to suffer. All she did was go to sleep."

Keeping the gun pointed directly at Tobin's chest, she went over to her mother, waggled out a hand, and felt for her mother's wrist.

Tobin kicked her very hard in the hip. It knocked her backwards onto the bed.

He grabbed the gun and then stumbled to the phone.

He shouted for somebody to send the doctor and the captain to the cabin where Susan Richards was being kept.

By the time he had turned back to the bed, the sobbing had begun, and what he saw then startled him.

Joanna Howard, very much like a child, clung to the unconscious form of her mother; clung as if to let go would be to fall down a dark chasm.

"How could you do that to me? How could you do

that to me?" she said over and over as she kissed Susan's face and stroked her hair as if her mother were a doll. "How could you do that to me? I'm your own daughter. Your own daughter." The rage was gone; there was just the sadness left, and the bafflement. As she said, she was Susan's own daughter.

Tobin went over and checked Susan's pulse again. He didn't tell Joanna—and Joanna didn't seem to realize—her mother, though comatose, was still alive. Several times on the cruise, Susan had asked Tobin to talk. Now he wished he'd spent the time.

He untied the steward. The man had cigarettes in his jacket pocket. Tobin took one and lit it and then went out on the deck. Joanna was still sobbing, still talking to the dying woman. He didn't want to hear anymore.

The captain and the doctor ran past.

Tobin stood at the railing and looked out at the black water and the sky. He wondered about the nature of god and the nature of man. Even from here he could hear Joanna crying.

He smoked his cigarette and in a time, without quite wondering why, he started crying too. He was thinking of that trailer and the yellow furious heat it must have cast against the black night, and the burned infant girl crawling away from it.

He stood at the railing, alone, for a long time.

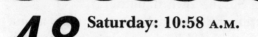

48

Saturday: 10:58 A.M.

They slept together and then Cindy went
back to her own cabin to shower and change.

When he found Cindy, she was sitting at a table with
a pink sun umbrella over her. He saw again the bruise
on the side of her face from where Joanna had struck
her. There was a glass of orange juice and an omelet
and two pieces of toast in front of her. She paid no
attention to them. She kept pulling up the falling left
strap of her sundress and writing heatedly (Balzac
must have composed this way, Tobin thought) on baby
blue stationery.

He ate half her toast and all of her eggs and drank
most of her orange juice before she looked up.

"Oh, gosh, Tobin."

"Hi."

"I was just writing to Aberdeen. About all the murders and everything and how I got slugged and how
Susan almost died and Joanna is under arrest. I was
really scared."

"Ah."

"Aberdeen just won't believe it. She really won't."

"I don't blame her."

"But she'll be thrilled."

"I'm sure." He had every reason to smile. He
phoned *Snoop* with the whole story. They had promised a bonus.

"She'll tell everybody in the insurance office and by the time I get back there, there'll even be something about it in the company newsletter."

"Should I be happy for you?"

"Nobody's ever put me in the company newsletter before."

"Then I'm happy for you."

"You don't sound happy."

He reached out and touched her sweet Kansas City hand. "It's not a morning to be happy," he said.

He thought about it all: Joanna and Susan and how they'd looked when the Coast Guard had taken them away; Cassie revealing that she'd been forced to pay Ken a special "talent fee"—another form of blackmail—to stay on "Celebrity Circle"; Sanderson and Iris Graves learning that the winner of a nowhere talent show in Indiana was actually Susan; Ken turning crazed and extorting money from his own accomplices in setting the trailer fire—and them being so afraid of losing their careers that they'd gone along.

She put down her ballpoint pen. "Look at the sun and the blue water, Tobin. Then you'll be happy."

He laughed. "You promise?"

"Sure," she said, laughing too. "I promise."

When a steward came by, Tobin ordered a rather large glass of orange juice, this one with some vodka in it, and then he sat back beneath the pink sun umbrella while Cindy went back to writing Aberdeen, and he looked at the yellow sun and the blue water and he tried very hard to be happy.

He tried very hard.